Autumn Winters

Realm Watchers Book 1

J. S. Malcom

Copyright © 2016 J. S. Malcom

ISBN-13:978-1537380087
ISBN-10:1537380087

CHAPTER 1

I'm trying to stay dry, waiting for the bus, when he joins me in the shelter. I glance over just long enough to register that he looks to be in his forties with longish dark hair. I avert my eyes to the advertisement taped to the glass behind him. The Soul Mites, whoever they are, played at the Canal Club three days ago. There's no reason to keep reading the flier but I do for a few seconds more before turning to look out at the street again.

He shuffles closer, his shoulder nearly touching mine as he too stares out. I consider stepping out from beneath the covering but the rain drums hard against the glass above and runs in torrents in the gutter. If it was raining lightly it might be worth it but I don't feel like riding home soaked.

He clears his throat and I feel him waiting for me to turn. I refuse. Partly because I take this bus often. I don't need him hanging out with me each time. And partly because I'm just not in the mood to hear his story. We all have stories and he can just keep his to himself.

"Think it's cold enough?"

In my peripheral vision, I see him blow on his hands. He wears a heavy coat when it's sixty degrees. He waits but I don't answer. One thing I've come to realize is that most of them don't know what's going on. In the beginning, I thought they'd have to but that's the rare exception. Most of them are lost, living in some other time. I wish I'd figured that out sooner.

I glance down Broad street, watching as the neon lights of bars and restaurants flicker to life. In half an hour, it will be fully dark. Cars zoom by as rush hour builds. People walk along the sidewalk, not noticing me as I watch them.

"They say it's supposed to snow tonight," the guy says. "Sure feels like it."

In the distance, thunder rumbles, which isn't unusual for September in Richmond as the summer storms linger. A mosquito whines at my ear and I try not to laugh. It's not funny, I know, but how can he not notice that I'm wearing a t-shirt and jeans? Obviously, he can see me.

"Who knows, maybe we'll have a white Christmas," the guys says. "They say the last time we had one here was in 1969. Man, that's like twenty years ago."

An image flashes into my mind—this same man, younger, driving a truck through some other town covered in snow. The glimpse into his past is fleeting, gone again almost immediately but with it comes a sense of sadness, an enduring regret. My heart goes out to him, it really does, but I remind myself that he has no idea. There's no sense in freaking him out by telling him that 1969 was almost fifty years ago. Or that we actually had a white Christmas here just a few years ago. It would just mess him up too much.

I turn at the sound of a rumbling engine and see that the bus just stopped at the light two blocks away. I check my phone and it's pushing seven o'clock.

"I like your earrings," the guy says.

"Thanks," I say, before realizing. Shit. I close my eyes and exhale.

He turns to face my profile. "I thought you could hear me."

Illogically, I shake my head, which only confirms the truth.

"You can. You can hear me!"

Brakes squeal and the bus lurches to a stop, wafting diesel exhaust into the air. The door opens with a pneumatic whoosh and I stride toward that opening. I don't look back until I grab a seat next to a middle-aged lady. She looks around to be sure I'm serious. After all, the bus is half empty. And, of course, if the bus stop guy followed me she wouldn't know.

But the bus gets moving and she goes back to staring at her phone. For now, she's stuck with me. She has no idea but it could be much worse. I tell myself not to look back but I can't help it. Thankfully, the guy remains at the bus stop. Maybe he didn't feel like going anywhere or maybe he just can't. I have no idea. It shouldn't surprise me when our eyes meet but some things just don't change. Each time, it surprises me. The bus keeps moving and I don't look back again.

~~~

The apartment is a mess—beer and wine bottles cluttering surfaces in the living room, dishes piled in the sink—which doesn't surprise me. After all, I live alone. I need to clean the place up, I tell myself. And I will. Later tonight. Maybe tomorrow. Right now, I need to chill for a few minutes. It gets to me every time, seeing them, trying to fake them out. There's nothing I can do to help them.

The cat door clatters and Louie hops into the room. He advances toward me, then stops to stretch his legs and yawn. He stares at me with his one eye, the missing one closed in a permanent wink. He carries a dead mouse between his teeth, which he deposits at my feet. A gift, timed for my arrival, his cat way of telling me that he's happy to see me. He wanders off into the apartment, not glancing back, confident now that I won't starve. I double-check to be sure he's gone, put the mouse into a sandwich bag and drop him in the trash. Poor little thing.

I check the fridge to discover that I'm down to one bottle of Rolling Rock. Great. I didn't think to stop at the store and now I'll have to go out again. I crack it open over the sink, looking at my reflection in the darkening kitchen window.

"You could try not drinking tonight," I whisper.

She stares back at me, this person I used to know—a pallid face framed with black hair, pale blue eyes and freckles across the bridge of her nose. "Yeah, right," she whispers back. Evidently, she knows me better than I know her.

I take my beer into the living room and clear a spot on the couch, moving last night's blanket aside. Many nights, I sleep out here. Not that I sleep well, even then, but I sleep better if I leave the TV on so I can hear people talking and laughing along with the occasional swell of music. If I'm lucky, those dwelling in the apartments around me might have friends over or even a party. Sounds of life. I rest better hearing those still living.

I flop down and throw my legs onto the coffee table. A beer bottle from last night topples, rolls and knocks down another. Thankfully, I don't accidentally throw a strike, which wouldn't be hard to do given my collection. No glass shatters so I'm good for now. That's about as optimistic as I get these days.

The room continues to grow dark, the streetlight in front of my apartment building casting a halo against my windows. I stare at the light reflected there as a memory comes to me, one from when I was only six years old. Even now, I'm not sure if it was a dream or something that actually happened. I remember light flickering against my eyes in the darkness and waking up to see Cassie sitting in her bed. At first, I thought it must be the glow of the moon creating the aura surrounding my little sister. I rubbed my eyes, then looked again as what was diffused took on the form of a shrinking sphere. I watched it descend toward Cassie's outstretched hands.

"What is that?" I whispered.

Cassie gazed down at the shimmering orb she now held in her open palms. If she heard me, she gave no sign of it as the room pulsed with soft, white light. Soon, the orb lifted into the air again, floating back toward the ceiling.

"Cassie?"

She turned in my direction as if just waking up. She looked right at me. The orb winked out and Cassie closed her eyes as she fell back against the bed. She breathed deeply, rhythmically, sound asleep again. A moment later, she rolled onto her side, facing away from me. I remained sitting in the darkness, staring off across the room for what felt like a very long time.

My phone buzzes against my thigh and I dig it out of my pocket. It's Molly, which is both the last thing I need and the thing I need most. Life's weird that way.

"Hey," Molly says. "How's it going?"

"Doing good." I sit up a little, glad that she can't actually see me.

Molly knows, of course, how completely I derailed after Justin died. Actually, everyone knows. I haven't exactly done a great job of hiding it. But she's the only one who knows about the things I see now.

"So, guess what?"

Molly sounds both nervous and excited. Somehow, I know what it is. That's another recent development, being able to know things. Like intuition except without the uncertainty, the self-questioning. When I know, I know, and this time it feels like the floor drops out from under me—my future that never happened unraveling again. Still, she has to tell me. We're best friends so sometimes we have no choice but to hurt each other.

I set my beer down and force myself to brighten my voice. "What's going on?"

"I wanted you to be the first to know," she says.

CHAPTER 2

After the call, it's just me sitting in the dark with my bottle of beer. I'm happy for Molly, I tell myself. I really am. She'll make a fantastic mother and life has to keep moving forward. That's just the way it works. I wouldn't want anything else for her.

I think back to when Molly told me she'd met someone, that it was the real deal. I was afraid I wouldn't like him but the minute I met Daniel —with his long, curly red hair and fingers stained from paint—I knew he was perfect for Molly, my friend the painter and sculptor. Justin got along with him too, from the moment they met. They liked the same kind of books, they were both fans of the Pixies, Kings of Leon and Muse, they loved going to Rams basketball games. Justin had just finished getting his master's degree in architecture and accepted a position with a firm downtown while Daniel was a econd-year graduate student at VCU Art. Even their disparate career paths didn't create a gulf between them. Those two hit it off so well that, as Molly and I planned our weddings, we used to joke that we'd get ditched and they'd run away together. But before long Molly and Daniel got married, of course. As did Justin and I, the weddings being within a month of each other two summers ago. It seemed inevitable that at some point the four of us would take the next steps of becoming parents. The future stretched ahead for us to share.

"So much for that plan," I whisper. Still, I raise my bottle to her in the dark, knowing how hard it must have been for her to tell me. "Good for you, Molls."

Life moves on and that's just the way it goes. For the living, of course. For the dead, it seems to go one of two ways. Either you cross over or you stay here, suspended for some reason. I don't know why. Maybe you were murdered, committed suicide, still love someone too much to let go or can't get past being angry about something. Maybe you became so attached to a place or thing that you hold on like a toddler afraid of losing your toy. These are my theories so far but my opinions could change. There are also those who simply don't know they're dead, souls already just barely living at the time when it happened. Maybe they were in a coma or wandering the streets in a deranged haze, each day just like the last and time already forgotten because nothing ever changed as the years stacked up on top of each other.

Then there are people like me, who just about crossed over but then came back. I've researched them, obsessing, reading books and whatever I could find online. Each time, their stories are similar—the tunnel, the feeling of peace wrapping itself around them. The white light ahead and sensing the presence of others they once knew being nearby, sometimes beckoning them forward. Except for in my case, there was one difference. I've never encountered anyone describing what I experienced.

Cars roll by outside, tires hissing against wet asphalt. Rain drizzles down the windows, reflecting the light of nearby buildings. In the distance, the wail of a siren rises into the night, telling the world that something bad just happened. That lonely, sad sound.

When it happened, Justin had just looked over at me and asked, "What do you think, babe?"

His catchphrase, always accompanied by his crooked grin and his green eyes checking mine. We should go to Hawaii next fall. How about we check out that new series everyone's talking about? We should snag concert tickets while we still can.

What do you think, babe?

We were driving back from the beach at night, cruising along a lonely stretch of 460. Justin had suggested we catch a train up to New York the next weekend, to see a play and spend a night in a Manhattan hotel.

"We could have an Italian dinner somewhere," he said. "Real Italian food. Spaghetti alle vongole, ravioli with vodka sauce. A bottle of red. Maybe some tiramisu and a very sweet espresso to keep us up for a while?"

I turned to see that crooked smile, Justin's face lit by an approaching car.

"What do you think, babe?"

The world exploded. A deafening punch of metal against metal. Glass fissuring in a suddenly blooming spider web. The burst of airbags scorching my skin. Lurching sideways, pinned by seatbelts as bones snapped and skin ruptured. The acrid smell of burning rubber stinging my nostrils. And blood, of course— Justin's running down his face and mine trickling into my eyes in the moments that followed. I remember that Justin's eyes were open, already glazed and distant.

At the time, I felt no pain. It happened too fast and there was too much to feel, no way to process it all. The body has limits, after all. We go numb. We shut down. Simultaneously short-circuit a million nerve endings and it's utter chaos. Think of it like a computer encountering a wall of incomprehensible code. It crashes, goes black.

Then came the feeling of rising. That's typical, I've come to know. People say that at first it feels like they're going up. Was I actually rising, I mean physically? I don't think so. I think that's the best my brain could do with what was going on. Next came another shift in perception, a leveling off as I moved forward through a tunnel toward a pulsing light. Of course, I wasn't seeing with my eyes anymore. I'd left them behind, closed tight, in that tomb of a car. I felt Justin next to me and I perceived him to be holding my hand even though, physically, that wasn't possible either.

Here's where things got different, something I've never heard of happening to anyone else. Where there had just been one light at the end of one tunnel, I now saw two. I felt Justin trying to hold on to me—I felt the force of his will, his love, trying to maintain the connection between us—but then that essence, that thing that was him, slipped away. I still felt warmth around me. Even a sense of peace, as if someone or something had stepped in to buffer the change.

But no explanation was offered. Justin was just gone and I heard a woman's voice. "I'm sorry," she said. "You have to go back."

I opened my eyes and it was three weeks later.

~~~

I suck back the last of my beer as Louie pads into the room and saunters toward me. He twists as he rubs his back against my leg. He purrs and I pick him up. I stare at his battered face, his one eye and torn ear. I have no idea what happened to him. That story took place before we met and he has no way to tell me.

"How's it going, sweetie?"

He blinks his eye patiently and I get it. This isn't about him, it's about me. He knew, in his animal way, and came to check on me.

"I'm okay," I tell him. "Really, I'm doing great."

Louie settles into my lap and starts licking his fur. His motor runs, his cat body vibrating. I swear, he's shaking the couch through me and he's not that big of a cat.

"Did I ever tell you about when I was little?" I say. "I used to like drawing. People, mostly. Faces, usually, but I was good at hands too. Everyone says they're really hard to draw."

Louie licks at his paws, his eye half closed. He's bored. Fair enough. I'm boring myself, avoiding the subject.

"Did I ever tell you about my sister? Her name was Cassie."

Louie scratches behind his ear. Yes, he's heard this story before. He cares but there's nothing he can do.

"Molly's pregnant," I say.

Louie stops purring, takes a moment, then hops off my lap. He wanders across the room, stopping to stretch and think, then hacks up a hairball before going into the kitchen. A moment later, the cat door rattles and I know he's gone back into the wild. I have almost no doubt that he'll bring back a gift later.

When I die, I'm taking Louie with me.

Good luck to anyone who tries to stop me.

CHAPTER 3

I throw on a light jacket, a ball cap and, like Louie, wander out into the wild. Well, there's only so much wild between my apartment and Rory's since it involves just a couple of miles on the bus. Sometimes I opt for walking, but it's still raining. Maybe I'll walk back later and grab a six-pack or a bottle of wine. Not exactly the best excuse for getting some exercise but that's probably what will happen.

Not lying to myself is rule number one. Obviously, I have to lie to other people. When someone asks how your day is going, you can hardly tell them that you were just talking to a dead guy at the bus stop. I've given that sort of thing a whirl a few times and it didn't go over well.

It's a Thursday so I'm not surprised to see that there's already a pretty good crowd building at Rory's. The place isn't packed yet, but it probably will be later. Rory's is one of those comfortable little neighborhood bars that's been around long enough to fit like an old, soft sweatshirt. You probably wouldn't wear that sweatshirt out on a date, but you're always happy to throw it on at the end of the day. I opt for one of the booths since I'm not really in the mood to strike up a conversation with one of the regulars perched at the bar. I can sit here and read a book on my phone or scroll through Facebook and Twitter. Of course, I should probably order something to eat since I'm taking up a booth. I used to work in restaurants too so I realize the value of prime tip-earning real estate.

"Hey, Autumn. Someone joining you?"

I look up from my phone to see Penny smiling at me. She's pushing forty, a divorced mother of two who's been working at Rory's since she was a hottie in her twenties. She married some lawyer, who later dumped her for a paralegal at his firm. Not surprisingly, the paralegal was the same age Penny had been when she and the lawyer first met.

"I was just in the mood for some quality me time," I say. "In a public place, that is."

Penny nods knowingly. "You wanted to be alone but not *alone*."

I sigh. "You might say that."

Penny gets it. One night, when she was closing the place and it was just the two of us, I decided to open up to her about my recently gained ability to see ghosts. Let's just say I'd overindulged a bit. But I had the feeling that Penny could handle it. She's always come across as being open-minded about things. As it turned out, my hunch was right. She'd never actually seen a ghost, but she used to feel her mother's presence after she'd passed away. She told me that they used to talk.

"Legend Lager?" Penny asks.

Legend Lager is my go-to beer when at Rory's since they don't carry Rolling Rock. "Sounds good. And maybe a menu."

Penny's nods but then adds, "You know, you tip better on two beers than most of these clowns do on a four course meal. Take the booth for as long as you'd like."

"You're the best," I say.

"Still want that menu?" Penny knows I don't exactly come here to eat.

I shrug and offer a smile. "Not really hungry."

"Didn't think so."

Penny delivers my beer and then another as the next hour passes. It's pushing ten o'clock and people keep wandering in. At one point, a guy claims a seat at the end of the bar and I can't help but notice him. Not in that way, not these days, although I guess at another time I would have taken an interest. He looks to be in his early-thirties, with the athletic build of someone who gained that physique naturally. He has an angled face with a nicely defined nose and prominent cheekbones. His wavy, chocolate hair might have seen a comb earlier but now appears carelessly tousled and his brown eyes occasionally glance up from beneath thick, arched brows. But while I notice him sitting there alone in a room full of people, he doesn't once look at me. Which I can't help but take a little personally. Why I still care is beyond me, but I do. I guess we're just hardwired that way.

After the crash, I looked bad for a while. Really bad. The emotional devastation accounted for most of it. You just can't go through something like that and not have it written on your face. But there was also the weight loss when I was thin to begin with. Three weeks in a coma makes for one hell of a diet. By the time I finally faced myself in a mirror, I looked like a warning ad about eating disorders. I've always looked young—more like a teenager than a woman in her twenties—but now I looked like an emaciated child.

The door opens again as more people spill into the room. They're young, a mix of male and female and I'm guessing they're probably VCU students. A lot of them live in the apartments nearby, and they like Rory's for cheap drinks. My eyes lock in on one of them right off. She's blonde and pretty, striking even, with her luminous blue eyes, straight nose and full lips. Despite the fact that she's wearing old jeans and a hoodie, I immediately think she could have been a model. Past-tense being the most important part of the thought. She should be drawing stares but a quick check of the room proves that nobody else sees her. Except one other person, maybe.

I look down at my phone, letting my hair fall around my face. I know ghosts and they can sense people like me. I'm not sure why. A matter of frequency, I guess. Something you're both dialed into. And here I am, sitting alone in a booth. I'll bet anything she slides in across from me within minutes because, to her, I'm a beacon. I'm a freaking lighthouse casting some beam I can't see out into the gap between this world and the next.

Before long, though, I sneak another glance, my curiosity too much. Yes, she's still there and the guy at the end of the bar is still watching her.

It seems incredibly unlikely, but he is.

The girl crosses the room, trying to talk to people who can't hear or see her. I wonder how much more horrible it must be to have once been stunning and now be invisible. It's cruel. Here she is hoping to get noticed when for her entire life it must have seemed utterly impossible not to be. Either way, it's only a matter of time before she locks in on me. I dig into my bag, take out a twenty, and leave it on the table. It's definitely time to head out.

CHAPTER 4

The rain has stopped, but fog crept in while I sat in Rory's. I walk through that fog now, the streetlights casting cones of luminescence that capture swirling mist. I should go straight home, but I really want a bottle of wine. J.J.'s Market is only two blocks off and I walk toward neon signs advertising beer and cigarettes, drawn like a moth. Not long ago, I was newly married, looking forward to finishing my MFA in Design with the hope of someday starting my own business. I barely drank and rarely got drunk. Now, I'm wandering around out here at night trying to avoid ghosts and unwilling to go home without alcohol because I'm afraid I won't sleep. My eyes start to prickle and I wipe the back of my hand across my face.

And, no, I'm not alone. I can't hear her behind me—her steps will never make sound again. All the same, I feel her there and soon she walks beside me.

"Hello?" she says.

I keep walking. God, it breaks my heart but I don't want her next to me.

"Can you hear me?"

Yes, I can hear you. I say nothing.

One block to go and maybe I'll just uncork that bottle right in the store. With any luck, she'll veer off and find some other lucky person to latch onto.

"I really need your help." Her breath hitches as her voice rises in pitch. She's also crying and I just can't ignore her—it's not about me anymore.

I slow down, then stop. I wipe my eyes, realizing that she's not the only one crying.

"Are you okay?" she says.

Seriously? Things have gotten that bad?

I take a deep breath to calm down. "I'm fine. Okay, I'm lying but I can deal with that later. What's going on with you?"

"I'm not dead," she says.

I turn to look at her. No, she doesn't look dead but many of them don't. Not to me, anyway. Some are more translucent while others appear basically the same as you and me, give or take the glow around them. That's not guaranteed either. People are all different, whether dead or alive. One of my new theories is that we all start out as "dead" before becoming "alive" again. Like a lightbulb switching on and off again here in this realm. I think it's a circular system. It seems an efficient use of energy. In this theory, ghosts are glitches. But this girl next to me isn't interested in hearing about my theories, which change daily anyway. She just wants to know what's going on.

I really don't want to go there right now but I'm stuck in this situation. I look at her young, beautiful face. Trusting eyes stare back at me.

"I'm really sorry," I say. "Did it happen fast? Was it a car crash or something?"

She shakes her head. "That's not what happened."

I don't want to take it to the next level but, evidently, I have no choice. "Did you commit suicide?"

That happens a lot too, I've come to learn. Suicide is a big one for getting you grounded. You cause that kind of pain and you just can't move on.

She shakes her head again. "No. Please, that isn't what happened."

I think for a moment, hesitating because I hate the dark stuff. I really don't want to know if she was murdered.

"I'm not dead," she says. "I swear. They took my body!"

My mouth opens but no words come out. I haven't been doing this very long and it's not like I'm an expert. All I can guess is that she's traumatized. Maybe it just happened tonight and she's confused.

"Can you help me?"

The strangest feeling comes over me, a buzzing of energy sparking within my veins. I want to tell her that I can help her, that I know just what to do, but I have no idea why. Again, I open my mouth to speak and come up short. I think for a moment, then say, "I'll be right back."

I'm trying to buy time, hoping she'll be gone when I get back. I don't know what just happened but I feel lightheaded, my skin still tingling as I go into the store. I decide to get a six-pack instead of the wine. Even then, I'm not sure that will be enough to get me through.

Javier stands behind the counter watching a miniature television, like most nights. He bought the store a couple of years ago and opts to work the nightshift for some reason that's none of my business. Insomnia maybe, or maybe being home alone just makes him feel too lonely. "Hey, Autumn," he says. "How's it going?"

I wonder if it reflects poorly on me, being on a first-name basis with a guy making a living by catering to people too messed up to shop at an actual grocery store. But maybe it's just my mood. "Hey, Javs," I say, and wander in the direction of the beer cooler.

I pretend to peruse the selection, knowing I'll buy Rolling Rock as always. The girl's words keep ringing in my ears and I tell myself she has to be confused. It makes no sense but I find myself thinking about Cassie. I just can't go there right now. Maybe when I'm home alone with the six-pack. Actually, almost always when I'm home alone with a six-pack. Thinking about my sister who suddenly vanished from my life fifteen years ago pretty much goes with the territory. Just not now.

I grab the six-pack along with a yogurt and a box of microwavable popcorn. I haven't eaten anything, and all I have at home is a dead mouse. I take my groceries to where Javier stares at the Steelers game on his little television. I pretend to watch for a moment too.

"How are they looking this year?" I say, not that I'm actually interested. Justin used to care about the Steelers. I'm just killing time to avoid a ghost.

"Not too shabby," Javier says. "They're clobbering Chicago tonight."

"Sweet. First game of the season?"

"That's next week. This is still pre-season."

"Oh, right." I glance out at the street.

Javier picks up on my distraction. "Everything okay?" He turns to look out.

The girl paces outside but, of course, Javier sees only passing cars.

"Yeah, sure. Everything's fine."

Javier rings up my purchases and I absently stare at the screen behind him. The television shifts to a commercial for local news to follow the game, an anchorwoman appearing on the screen. I prepare to tune her out. There's nothing more depressing than local reporting, a procession of sordid crimes and fatal accidents, but the anchorwoman's words sink in and my eyes snap to the image being displayed—a photo of the girl I was just speaking to outside.

A search is underway tonight for a missing twenty-one year old Henrico woman. Rachel Joyner's disappearance was reported earlier this evening to local authorities when the Virginia Commonwealth University student—

"No lime?" Javier says, breaking my connection with the screen behind him.

"I'm sorry?"

"Usually, you get a lime." Javier raises his eyebrows, reminding me that he started stocking a few limes in his cooler because I asked him to one night. Weird, I know, but I like lime in my Rolling Rock.

"I'm good." My eyes flick back to the screen but they've moved onto other highlights for what's coming later.

"Thirteen, fifty-nine," Javier says.

"Huh? Oh, right." I dig in my bag and hand him my debit card.

Now I want to get back outside, when before it was the last thing on earth I wanted to do. Oh, my God, she's still missing. No one knows what happened to her.

I search the window as I walk toward the door. Outside, cars and buses zoom past. Other people are on the sidewalks but I see no sign of the girl. I feel sick to my stomach. How much longer will she have to wander around out there thinking she's still alive? Maybe if I could have convinced her that she's dead she could have helped me locate her body. That way, at least her parents would know the truth. Now, there's nothing I can do and I fight back tears as I look around once more. That's when I spot him across the street, the same guy I saw in the bar. Our eyes meet just briefly before he turns and walks off in the opposite direction.

CHAPTER 5

Molly and I have arranged to meet at the Urban Farmhouse on Broad, a place she can get to quickly for her break between classes. As I approach, I see her sitting at a table by the front window. She's looking at her phone and frowning. I check my own to see that I'm twenty minutes late. Not cool. Molly told me she only has an hour. But I've been distracted lately, can't seem to get my act together since the other night. I can't stop thinking about Rachel Joyner, not to mention that guy I saw. I keep telling myself it was just a coincidence, him being outside the store. That he wasn't watching me. Why would he? Still, I can't quite shake the feeling he was doing just that.

Molly looks up and smiles as I enter the café. If she's annoyed, she does a good job of hiding it. But that's one of the perks of having your life go totally to hell. People try not to act mad at you. Of course, this is also the first time I've seen her since she told me she's pregnant. So, the pity factor just went up another notch when neither of us imagined it possible so soon.

"Hey, Molls," I say, taking a seat across from her.

Her eyes show that I probably don't look good. It's just one of those things about having a friend since you were fifteen—she can size me up at a glance. "Bought you a latte," she says. "Got you a double just in case."

"Good thinking. Thank you." Although, what I'm thinking is that I might have opted for a glass of wine. Like I haven't been drinking enough lately.

I pour in some sugar and give it a stir. "You look great."

And she does. Molly's skin glows and her eyes shine with health and happiness. My words catch her sipping her coffee and she swallows, then wipes her mouth with her hand. "You too," she says.

I level her with a knowing look. "You seem to be forgetting that I have several mirrors in my apartment."

Molly laughs, then shrugs. "Okay, maybe you look a little tired. But I like your shirt."

"Oh, right. You gotta love Etsy." Which I do. Where else could you find a one-eyed cat t-shirt?

One of the baristas shows up at our table, a guy wearing jeans, a black apron and bearing two brownies. "Here you go, guys," he says, offering a smile and a display of inviting dimples.

"Whoa, look at that," I say, as he leaves again.

Molly swivels in her chair to watch him go, then turns back to me with a raised eyebrow.

I shoot her a deadpan look. "I meant the brownies."

Molly glances at the barista again. "Now, I'm thinking I'd rather have the cupcakes."

Just like that, I find myself laughing for what feels like the first time in weeks. That's the thing about Molly. When

I'm with her, it takes maybe five minutes before we revert to being teenagers. Damn, it feels good to be around her again. I remind myself that there's a reason I stay away these days. For her sake, not mine.

I check out the brownies and they really do look amazing. They warmed those suckers up too, I can tell from the aroma. "I haven't even had lunch yet," I say, tearing off a chunk.

"So, now you're having lunch." Molly picks up her brownie and takes a bite. "Doing okay?"

It's really the only question she can ask. Molly knows what I'm about these days.

I shrug. "Sure, doing fine."

She nods and takes another bite of her brownie. Molly's way of not saying what I know she's thinking—that, by now, I should have gone back to school. After the accident, everyone understood why I bailed on everything while I got back on my feet. But it's been almost a year. The fact is, if Justin hadn't signed on for life insurance at work—something I told him was ridiculous at the time—I would have been forced to do something by now.

"I've been wondering," I say. "Do you think you'll still look for a job?" We have to go there sooner or later. We might as well go there now.

Molly looks down for a moment, then her eyes meet mine. "I'm sorry." The words just come out and I know she didn't mean to say it. But it's true, she's sorry. And she shouldn't be. I don't want her to feel that way.

Molly's eyes glisten and in ten seconds I know a tear will be rising to my eye as well. A moment of silence stretches between us before I reach across the table and take her brownie.

Molly does a double-take.

"Do you want your brownie back?" I keep my eyes on hers.

Molly considers, then nods, the corners of her mouth lifting in a smile.

"Be sure about this," I say. "Because this is a very important decision." I inch her brownie even closer to my own.

"Yes," Molly says. "I really want my brownie back."

"Then don't ever tell me you're sorry, not about this."

"Okay."

"You're sure about that?"

Molly nods.

"Good. Because I plan to enjoy every minute of being your daughter's crazy aunt, or whatever it is I'll be to her. And don't ask me how I know it will be a girl. I just do. Don't ruin this for me. Okay?"

"I'm sorry." Molly's eyes go wide and she says, "Shit! I didn't mean it like that. I meant—crap, you know what I mean. Give me my brownie back."

I slide the plate and Molly snatches it back the rest of the way. We both start laughing.

"A girl?" Molly says. "You think so?"

She already knows that along with the ghost thing came a bit of something else. "You okay with that?"

Molly looks me in the eye. "Why? It's not like you can change it, right?"

"Definitely not that talented." I take a sip of my latte, which tastes great. Suddenly, a glass of wine is the very last thing I want. What I want is more of this. Daylight. Life. Happiness. It can happen, I know, even if sometimes it doesn't feel that way. They say you never get over it, but you do get used to it. It was the same with Cassie. If you're going to survive, you have to at least let yourself get used to it. From there, you can start to let daylight in again, a little at a time.

"By the way, she's going to hate you when she hits middle school," I say.

Molly's eyes go wide again.

I shake my head. "Not a prediction. That's just the way it usually goes."

"Right," Molly says. "Oh, crap. That's right around the time I decided my aunt was so much cooler than my mother."

I raise an eyebrow. "My evil plan has been launched. Now I just have to wait thirteen years to see if it works out."

We're still talking twenty minutes later, almost out of time before Molly's next class, when two girls come in. They're young, undergrad students obviously, from the way they're dressed and their backpacks.

"It's freaking scary," one of them says. "A guy in one of my classes works with her at Percolator, that new coffee place on Grace Street. He said she was literally right in front of him one moment and then she was gone."

I lock in on their conversation.

"Wait," her friend says. "They said on the news that she'd left and was on her way home or something."

They get in line behind a few others waiting for their orders to be taken. "That's not what happened," the first girl says. "Gary said they were just getting ready to leave when suddenly it was like the light went all weird. Then she just vanished."

"What does that even mean? Was he like high or something?"

My blood goes cold and I think I must have heard wrong. I slept like crap and I'm imagining things. I have to be.

Molly locks her eyes on mine. "Hey, are you okay?"

I hesitate, then say, "Yeah, I'm fine."

"They were talking about that girl, weren't they? I heard something about that on —" Molly stops and cocks her head. "Wait, did you...?"

I nod.

"Shit. When?"

"Last night."

I know sometimes Molly isn't sure what to think about the whole seeing ghosts thing. I understand. It's weird as hell. This time, though, I get the feeling she doesn't have any doubts.

"The poor thing," she says. "I hope they find her."

Not that I blame her—since it all happened before we met and I did my best not to bring it into our friendship— but Molly's making the mistake of assuming that Rachel Joyner will be found. Hopefully alive but the other implication is there too. It seems that, in this moment, Molly's forgetting something about my own past. Sometimes people just disappear. And, sometimes, no one ever finds them again.

~~~

I hadn't planned on going to Rory's that night but, then again, I don't typically plan on going to Rory's. It just sort of happens when I get sick of being around myself. In other words, it happens often. Tonight, though, I'm going there for a different reason. I can't stop thinking about that conversation I overheard.

She was literally right in front of him.

The light went all weird. Then she just vanished

I keep telling myself that can't be what I heard. Probably the guy they were talking about really was high or something. Or maybe he was confused, upset about what happened. It has to be some sort of coincidence. Nothing to do with what happened to my sister.

Still, I keep wondering why Rachel Joyner came to Rory's the other night. True, ghosts can pop up anywhere but, in my experience, they tend to stay around what they knew, both places and people. Had she been looking for someone?

It's still early when I get there so the place isn't Friday night crazy yet. Even so, a number of barstools and booths are already occupied. Penny's behind the bar, maybe finishing her day shift or covering until the night bartender gets there.

"Hey, Autumn," she says, as I take a seat at the bar. "Whatcha having?"

"I guess a glass of red." I don't have to be any more specific since Rory's only has two kinds of wine, cabernet or chardonnay. Thankfully, the cabernet isn't too bad.

Penny brings the wine a minute later. "You look like crap," she informs me.

I have to laugh. Leave it to Penny to be honest.

"My neighbors were having a party last night," I tell her, since sometimes it doesn't seem fair burdening her with updates from the world of ghosts. Penny's a good listener, but I don't want to wear out my welcome.

The door opens and Penny looks to see who's coming in. I watch in the back-bar mirror, two couples engaged mid-conversation, smiling and laughing as they slide into one of the booths.

Penny sighs and I don't think it's just because she doesn't feel like taking on more customers. Happy people are just painful to watch. I want to reach out and pat the back of her hand, promise her that love will happen again. True love this time with someone who'll keep her laughing and smiling for the rest of her life. I really hope that happens but, while I'm a little bit psychic, I'm not that psychic. I have no idea what the future holds for Penny. So, I say nothing as she puts her pad in her apron and sets off, menus in hand.

With Penny gone, I scan the back-bar mirror to see who sits alongside me tonight. There's a one-stool gap to my right and then two women, probably on the late side of thirty. One of them looks mildly distraught and the other appears to be delivering some sort of pep talk. My guess, a job issue. The distraught chick doesn't display glistening eyes and her friend appears only half-interested as she glances at her phone while delivering encouragement. Of course, she could just be a crappy friend. Past them, an older man stares up at the silent TV which, as usual, is tuned into ESPN. I glance to my left, past a two-stool gap this time. Two guys and a girl, probably in their mid-twenties, sit talking as a group. Past them, at the end of the bar, I see a young guy sitting alone. I guess he must be twenty-one to be in here since Penny doesn't mess around when it comes to IDs. The kid looks like a teenager, though, as he grasps his pint of beer and stares down at the bar. He senses me watching and looks up. Our eyes meet before I look away again, but I'm pretty sure he's one of the college kids from the other night.

Penny comes back behind the bar after delivering drinks to the table full of happy people. "Wow, that was fast," she says, eyeballing my now empty glass.

There's honest and there's too honest, which might be why Penny is better off not tending bar full-time. There's a certain level of diplomacy involved that she hasn't exactly mastered.

I shrug. "Like I said, I didn't sleep well. Why don't I buy one for the young man over there too." I nod in the direction of the kid drinking solo.

Penny's brow creases slightly, confusion registering in her expression.

No, Penny. I'm not planning to hit on him. "He looks a little down," I say.

Penny nods. "Yeah, I noticed. He looks like his dog died or something."

I'm thinking it might not be his dog but I just let her deliver the kid's beer. He looks up to search me out in the mirror again but I'm already claiming the spot next to him.

"Mind if I join you?"

He shrugs as if to say *It's not like I could stop you.* "Thanks for the beer."

"No problem. If you'd rather be alone, just say the word."

He thinks about that for a moment. "No, it's cool. I've been kind of keeping to myself all day as it is."

I take a sip of my wine. Just a sip. Penny's comment might not have been entirely appreciated but it wasn't exactly unwarranted. "I know how that goes. Sometimes, you just need a little time to think things through."

"Exactly," the kid says. "I'm Ed, by the way."

I shake his hand. "Autumn. I'm guessing you probably go to VCU."

He nods. "Third year. How'd you know?"

"I saw you come in last night with a bunch of your friends."

34

His eyes go distant suddenly, like I touched a nerve.

"Everything okay?" I say. "It's not like you guys were bothering anyone."

He shakes his head, as if to clear it. "It's not that. Something happened last night. I just didn't know it when we were here."

I wait, confused but not as much as he might think.

He takes a pretty impressive gulp of his beer before continuing. "A friend of mine went missing."

"That's horrible. No wonder you seem upset."

Ed nods and looks down at the bar.

I pretend to think for a moment. "Wait, are you talking about the girl who's been on the news?"

He nods. "Right, Rachel."

"Have they found out anything?"

"No. Not yet anyway. The whole thing's just weird. I mean, she went to her classes and then went to work later. She was supposed to meet up with us here but nobody heard from her. I should have called her." He takes another drink and runs his hand through his hair. "The thing is, Rachel could be a little flighty so no one really worried about it. To be honest, I figured she probably just flaked on us."

"That's understandable," I say. His eyes show how much he's been worried and the last thing he needs is guilt. I know better than anyone how much people blame themselves when this kind of thing happens.

Ed turns to look at me. "Can I tell you something?"

I keep my eyes on his, seeing a world of pain in his expression. He cared about Rachel, no doubt about it. "Sure, of course."

"This might sound weird but last night, when we came here…" He taps his forefinger on the rim of his glass. "Like I said, I didn't know anything about it yet. I keep telling myself it had to be my imagination. But I kept getting this really weird feeling."

He stops talking, and I get the feeling he's having second thoughts about saying more. I hate to press him but this whole thing has just been nagging at me too much. "What kind of a weird feeling?"

His gaze meets mine again. "I don't know how to explain it but I just kept thinking about her, like something wasn't right. And I kept getting the feeling she was right here next to us. I know that must sound crazy."

I can't bring myself to tell him that he's actually right. He'd think I'm insane. "I guess you were just worried about her."

"I was worried about her. I couldn't stop thinking about her. Then later I found out that she disappeared. It doesn't make any sense."

"I'm really sorry," I say again. "It must be hard to process something like that."

He locks his eyes on mine again. "No, I mean it literally doesn't make sense. There's stuff that hasn't been on the news. They questioned this guy who worked with Rachel. Gary Draper. They took him in for a polygraph, the whole deal."

There it is, I think. The crazy guy I heard those girls talking about earlier. It's just a matter of time now until the world hears the twisted story, most likely about some kid's obsession with a beautiful girl. How when she ignored him, his darker nature took over. They'll say he was quiet, that he hardly ever talked to anyone, but no one ever thought he'd be capable of doing something like this.

"Do you think he had something to do with it?" As I say it, I realize that my pulse has escalated. A million times over, I've thought about what might have happened to my sister and each time is as bad as the last. Fifteen years hasn't made any difference.

Ed shakes his head. "He's already out," he says. "Thank God, for once the cops didn't let the media get hold of it. They would have ruined his freaking life. I've talked to Gary at parties and stuff. There's just no way. He's a good guy."

I breathe a sigh of relief, my stomach starting to untwist from the repugnant scenario I just imagined. "What did he say?"

Ed shakes his head again, trying to make sense of things. "It has to be shock or something. I mean, who's going to believe some story about seeing lights and Rachel suddenly vanishing? No wonder they took the guy in for questioning."

~~~

I let myself into my apartment, still shaken from what I've now heard twice in one day. I keep telling myself that Ed has to be right. That his friend, Gary, must have been

37

dealing with shock. That somehow, in a million to one chance, the kid imagined something way too close to the bone for me. But what bothers me just as much is that I completely know how no one believes a story about your eyes going hazy and the light around you suddenly shifting at the very moment when someone vanishes. They definitely didn't believe me, that's for sure.

I sit down on the couch and hunch forward, holding my head in my hands as my hair falls around my face. I try not to think about it but it's not like I have a choice.

As it has a million times before, my mind jumps back to that night when Cassie and I ran down to the park at sunset. It was almost summer and we were hoping to see fireflies soon start rising into the night. I was finally old enough to take her and she was still young enough to enjoy using the swings. I remember thinking that, in another year, she'd be twelve and that would probably be that. Maybe we'd still go for walks but just as likely she'd tune into her phone or computer the same as I usually did. I remember thinking how much I'd miss going there because, even though there was no way I was going to sit on the swings anymore, it felt nice remembering when I did. I remember thinking about how I hadn't really wanted to take the stuffed animals out of my room but did anyway after one of my friends made fun of me. In other words, I was almost thirteen. Finally, almost a teenager and now part of me already missed being a kid.

It felt like it was going to rain and I told Cassie we'd probably get soaked walking back. She did that thing she used to do, planting her hand on her cocked hip and smirking. "What's it gonna do? Ruin your hair or something?"

I laughed because she was right. Who cared if we got caught in the rain walking back? At least, we'd have gotten out of the house for a while. And it wasn't like either one of us felt like doing our homework, especially with summer just about to start.

There were just the two of us there that night. Cassie on the swings and me wondering if I might be able to rescue my stuffed animals from the box in the garage. A drop of rain hit my nose and then another hit my forehead. Cassie was in mid-air, at the top of the swing's arc when I looked up at her. I remember that my skin started to tingle and I thought about lightning.

"We should probably go," I said.

That's when it happened. The buzzing pulse against my eyelids. The flickering.

After it happened, I told them that my eyes went funny. That my vision went suddenly blurry. That's all I could remember. I couldn't explain it then and I can't explain now. Over time, I've sometimes thought I remember more. I've imagined myself standing frozen in place as if unable to move. I've told myself that I heard someone speaking, a woman, but that doesn't make sense. It had to have been Cassie. We were all alone. All I knew then and all I know now is that my sister was there and then she was gone. And when my vision cleared again, I stood watching as an empty swing completed its arc back toward the ground.

A siren howls in the distance as an emergency vehicle rushes past on the street below. I straighten up, push my hair back and take a deep breath. I'm alone and I don't want to be. I so much don't want to be alone. I walk toward the kitchen, realizing that I forgot to stop at J.J.'s. After what that kid Ed said about weird lights and vanishing people, I just had to get home. Do I have any beer or wine? Yes, I do, I'm pretty sure. There has to be something. There has to be.

It's only then, as I make my way through the apartment, that I realize something doesn't feel right. I look around to be sure but there are no dead rodent or bird gifts left for me to pick up. There's no Louie stretched out anywhere and I haven't seen him all day. Louie's a free spirit but he's consistent in some things, one of them being touching base with me even if he gets bored ten seconds later and takes off again.

I flick on the kitchen light. "Louie?"

I double back, checking the dining room and bedroom. I return to the kitchen, to be sure I didn't leave anything blocking the cat door. I did that once, left a big box there by mistake, and Louie avoided one-eye contact for days.

When was the last time I saw him? I suddenly realize I don't know. Wasn't it last night? It must have been. But now I'm not so sure. I got home late and not exactly sober. I took a shower and spent what was left of the night on the sofa, hoping to get some sleep. In the kitchen, I check his bowl and it's still full. Not a good sign. I have no idea what

Louie catches and eats on his own but he almost always eats the food from the dispenser.

I open the back door and step out onto the landing. It's dark out there and at first everything looks normal. I reach back inside, flick the light on, and that's when I see him. I start to tremble, hoping I'm wrong but even now he doesn't stir.

"Come on, baby," I say, crouching next to him. "Come on, Louie. What's going on?"

Louie's curled up into a ball, fetal, his front paws covering his face. I tell myself he's just asleep but Louie never sleeps out here unless it's sunny. Either way, he never curls up like this. Louie stretches out confidently as if to claim as much space as possible. Still, he's asleep, I tell myself. He has to be asleep.

I try again. "Come on, baby. Come on, Louie. Do you hear me?"

He doesn't move. His one eye, now glazed and milky, stares at nothing.

I tell myself not to cry but it's already too late and I wipe my eyes with my arm. "No, no, no, Louie. Come on. Someday maybe but just not now, okay? You can't die on me!"

Still, I can't bring myself to touch him because I know what it will mean. I go back into the apartment, gasping like the world just ended, and I don't fucking care if anyone hears me sobbing. To anyone else, Louie might just seem like some old cat. They can't possibly know that, for some reason, he adopted me at the very point in my life when I felt most alone. I grab a towel from the closet, go back out to the porch and use it to scoop him up. I hug Louie's wrapped body to my chest and go back inside. I stand there with tears running down my face, rocking back and forth, holding him close. Finally, I bring myself to touch him, knowing I never will again. I run my hand over his head, petting him like he sometimes allowed me to do.

Then I feel it again, like last night. A current running through me, like sparks in my veins. Heat radiates from my chest and down through my arms. Suddenly, light flashes from my hand against Louie's fur. I gasp and rear back as he thrusts his legs against me, his claws suddenly piercing my shirt. Louie's head snaps in my direction, and he stares for less than a second. Then he leaps from my arms and shoots out the door.

CHAPTER 6

Paul walked through the night, striding slowly forward, not lowering his head or protecting himself from the rain. The fact was, he liked feeling it against his skin. Despite everything, the novelty never completely wore off. As he walked past the cozy glow of bars and restaurants, no one looked up although he was plainly visible beneath the streetlights. It had been a long time since he'd been noticed as being anything other than what he appeared to be. This, in Paul's mind, was as it should be.

He passed another business, a coffee shop this time. He slowed and looked in to see soft light cast by wall sconces, rows of books resting on shelves and the inviting glow of a gas fireplace. Strains of classical music floated into the night as a departing customer opened the door, the elegant sound muting again as the door swung closed. Couples sat gathered at tables, gesturing and smiling as they talked. Men and women relaxed in soft leather chairs, some typing into their machines and others gazing at their devices. Paul couldn't help but notice how refined they all appeared, despite their manner of dress or hairstyle, sophisticated and gentle in one another's company.

This too was as it should be, that they'd conquered their instinctive fears, banished any threats the night might hold from their conscious attention. Circumstances had once been quite different. Not so long ago, these same creatures had believed in demons, magic and monsters. Evil forces in the darkness just barely held at bay. They hadn't been wrong.

Paul reached the end of the square, leaving those nocturnally flourishing businesses behind. He stood waiting at a crosswalk, a light flashing against his eyes as he obeyed the law. He still heard faint stanzas of music—the rising swell of strings, the bass vibration of percussion, the swirl of woodwinds. The faint murmurings of conversation hummed in his ear. The light changed and he proceeded across a street devoid of traffic, past the ancient church with its cemetery full of faded headstones. Soon, he entered the park beyond.

As he continued through the cool, wet night Paul thought of the place he'd left long ago. A world where the elements were no longer left to chance, where rain and snow fell in a manner both controlled and regulated, their cycles not predicted but scheduled. His thoughts turned to gleaming cities, sword-like spires of glass and metal glittering against a violet sky. He pictured another sophisticated race of people, not so very different, really, from those he observed here each day.

That he found himself thinking of home once again, after so long, didn't really surprise Paul. The resonances he'd felt lately—which so rarely occurred in these times— could really only result in him considering one of two things. First was the place he'd given up in choosing to cross between realms, that world lost to him now. The other was the possibility of facing mortality again, that very same prospect which coming here had allowed him to avoid.

Someone fell in beside him but Paul didn't have to look over to know it was Claudia. For one thing, she knew the pattern of his nighttime walks. She also made barely a sound, moving with the preternatural grace typical of their kind despite the fact that, outwardly, she appeared to be a woman in her forties. Claudia fit the mold nicely for the identity she'd currently chosen to adopt—a middle-aged insurance agent with an uncanny skill for convincing people to purchase life policies. In fact, Claudia did quite well financially, something of a game to her since, after all, there wasn't any need. All the same, Paul couldn't help sometimes feel a bit jealous that she was so much more gifted at pretending. At fitting in. Then again, this was the only home she'd ever truly known. Looking back on his own recent choice, Paul wondered if it might have made more sense to select a face more likely to put people at ease. But the options had been limited at the time.

"Don't you think it's a bit cliché," Claudia said. "I mean, really. The dark, the rain, the cemetery."

Paul chuckled. "I enjoy the history. You know that."

Paul really did admire the history of the city he currently lived in. So many conflicts and shifts in such a short time. Relatively speaking. Less than two-hundred years ago, most of it had been set on fire. Now, here they were, not far from the resting places of some who'd died in the same conflict. In the time that had passed, a whole new city had bloomed and Paul had been there to watch it grow.

"By the way, you're soaking wet."

Paul had all but forgotten the rain until Claudia stopped it by covering him with her umbrella. "Thank you," he said. "Although I really didn't mind."

"I think you just have a flair for the dramatic," Claudia said.

This time Paul laughed, the sound of it incongruous to the setting. And possibly frightening, he imagined, should anyone else be out there with them. Paul highly doubted that was the case, given that he would almost have certainly sensed any other nearby beating hearts.

"I felt it," Claudia said. "Earlier tonight. Is that why you're out here prowling around?"

Paul knew what she meant, of course. She'd also picked up on the resonances. Paul felt sure they all must have. As had happened fifteen years ago, although those resonances had been subtle, little more than a rippling of the pond to foreshadow what would have come. They'd also been silenced swiftly as if someone had been waiting, listening for just that very phenomenon to occur. Paul had little doubt about who that might have been.

"I suppose you must have someone watching her," Claudia said.

Paul glanced over at her, meeting her gaze. She'd done this world a favor by allowing a new intelligence to reside behind those dark eyes. "Of course," he said.

"Which means they do as well."

"I'm sure. Although, I wonder if she's already too much of a threat, especially after what we felt tonight."

"A threat which we can't exactly ignore."

They rounded another curve in the path, their circling of the park nearly complete. Above, a sliver of moonlight cut through parting clouds. Claudia withdrew the umbrella, the rain having all but stopped.

"I'm afraid not," Paul said. "Before, that might have been possible even despite her proximity. As it is, they've more or less forced our hand."

"Why did her powers lay dormant this long?"

This was something Paul had also wondered about. "Trauma, possibly. Or it could be that her sister would have helped her make the connection."

Claudia nodded, giving Paul the impression she might have considered the same possibilities. "You're sure there's no way for her to know what she is?"

For the longest time, their kind had lacked the means to recognize their legacy. They'd been essentially erased from human history, consigned to the realms of fantasy and superstition. "Ironically, that's the crux of the problem," Paul said. "We'll need to make a decision."

They'd nearly reached the park entrance again, the street before them gleaming from the rain that had fallen.

"Soon," Claudia said. "But probably not tonight." Her way of telling him not to worry, that there was no reason for him to be wandering around in the rain.

Paul's gaze went to a distant light he'd passed before, his ears already picking up on the music and sound of people talking. "True," he said. "Should we have a coffee?"

"A coffee sounds nice," Claudia said.

Together, they continued to walk toward where others had gathered. They'd join them soon, looking for all the world as if they belonged there too.

CHAPTER 7

After what happened, sleep is basically out of the question. I think about running to hide at Rory's but, for once, I don't feel like drinking. I need to stay sober so I can figure out just what the hell is going on. I fill the kettle and set that on the stove to boil, then sit at the table. I run my hand through my hair and blow out through pursed lips. Well, shit.

Part of me wonders if I'm losing my mind. That would be the easiest explanation. It would explain so very much. I honestly can't say that I'm not but, from where I'm sitting, everything seems real enough. Too real. I flash back to seeing Louie's curled up form on the back porch, calling out to him, then picking him up. I know—I absolutely know—he was dead. And maybe if it wasn't for all the other weird shit going on in my life, I'd be able to convince myself it was just some sort of feline medical miracle. Except there hadn't been any medical intervention involved. What there had been was a sudden surge through my body and that light pulsing from my hands before Louie sprang back to life. It was me. I felt it.

In that moment, a memory comes rushing back at me—not one I forgot but one I've managed not to think about for a while. Now, I see that morning vividly once again. I'm nine years old, Cassie seven. It's a weekend and we're up early while our parents remain sleeping. Cassie and I are out in the family room watching cartoons—the Powerpuff Girls, even that part I remember clearly. I'm sitting on the floor drawing pictures, even then trying to master the seemingly impossible task of drawing realistic hands and faces.

Cassie sits on the sofa, dipping crackers into a container of peanut butter. She's surrounded by crumbs, undoubtedly smearing oil into the upholstery with her fingers, and I just know my mother is going to kill her. But it's not like I'm worried about it, not enough to do anything. It's not me who's going to get in trouble. I lower my head back to my drawing and that's when I hear Cassie cry out.

"Autumn, look!"

I glance up to see Cassie staring at the aquarium. It's on a stand by the window, where sunlight streams through the glass past pink castles and plastic seaweed. That's what I see first but Cassie gets up and walks toward it, her arm outstretched as she points.

"What' wrong with Dolphin?"

The aquarium was Cassie's birthday gift and she named the two goldfish, Dolphin and Sandy.

I know right off but I'm not sure how to tell her. "He's probably just resting," I say, hoping she'll go back to watching the Powerpuff Girls.

"He's upside down!" Cassie says. "Come here!"

I get up off the floor and go to stand next to her. I stare into the water where Sandy swims in lazy circles, oblivious to the fact that the sole fellow inhabitant of his small world now floats belly up on the surface.

There doesn't seem any point in faking it any longer. "I think he's dead."

Cassie swivels her head and stares into my eyes. "He can't be dead. We just got him."

"It doesn't work that way."

"He can't be dead!" Tears start to stream down Cassie's cheeks and she points her small finger again. "Look, he's still moving!"

"He's just floating around in the bubbles," I say.

Cassie shakes her head. "No he's not. He's moving. I'll make him okay again."

She wipes her hands on her pants and reaches toward the water.

"Ew, don't touch him! Cassie, he's dead!"

Cassie reaches into the aquarium and scoops up the dead fish. I wince against a sudden flash, what I think must be sunlight on rippling water. The fish in Cassie's hand twitches, then flips. Cassie shrieks and drops him back into the water. Dolphin dodges past Sandy to swim a quick circle around the tank.

I burst out laughing. "Holy shit!"

Cassie's eyes go wide. "You just swore! I'm telling!"

But then she starts laughing too. And we keep laughing as we continue to watch Dolphin and Sandy swim circles around each other in the early morning sunlight.

~~~

It's been a long time since I just dropped in on my mother without calling first. Actually, it's been a long time since I visited at all. It's not that we don't get along—we do, well enough all things considered. We talk fairly often. The fact is, though, it's difficult facing her. She doesn't even have to say anything for me to know I'm a total mess these days. I can just see it in her eyes.

My mother works at a bank, Tuesdays through Saturday, so if her schedule hasn't changed she should be off today. I drive through the neighborhood she lives in now. When my parents got divorced, they sold the old place where Cassie and I grew up together. Well, almost grew up together. That was a nice neighborhood full of Colonial homes on large lots, surrounded by old growth trees. We had a neighborhood pool and tennis courts. It was the kind of place where neighbors took to the cul-de-sacs on holidays like Memorial Day and the Fourth of July for block parties. Everyone lit luminaries on Christmas Eve and lined those glowing white paper bags with candles inside them along the streets in front of our houses.

Maybe I'm romanticizing the old neighborhood, but there's no doubt that the one my mother lives in now is a little on the shabby side. It's still in the suburbs but closer to the city, with smaller houses—old tri-levels and ranches built in the seventies—crowded close together. Some display motor homes in the driveway, others cars on blocks. All in all, it's a little depressing. What's weird, is that as I park in the driveway, I momentarily feel thankful that Cassie never got to see it. Which makes no sense, of course, and I remind myself that if she hadn't gone missing my mother wouldn't be living here alone and my father wouldn't have drank himself to death.

I ring the doorbell and, only then, remember that I didn't take a shower or bother to brush my hair. Not to mention, I was in a cold sweat the entire time I was driving since it's been months since I got behind the wheel. I lean past the door to see myself in the doorframe windows and I'm running my fingers through my tangled hair when my mother emerges from the back of the house. She sees me and her eyes widen with something close to shock. She's a middle-aged woman living alone and she'd probably find more comfort in discovering a total stranger at her door. I had just enough time to see my own pale skin and the dark circles under my eyes. Yes, I look like hell.

"Great, this is going to be fun," I mutter under my breath.

By the time my mother opens the door, she's managed to compose herself. She keeps her eyes on mine and smiles. "Hi, honey. Come in!"

I do and she shuts the door behind me.

"What a nice surprise," she says. "What are you doing here?"

Saying that I was just in the neighborhood isn't exactly going to work. At the same time, it doesn't seem fair to clobber her over the head with why I came here. Which, as far as I know, might only further convince her, and possibly myself, that I'm losing it.

"You said I could have some of the old dishes. Are those still boxed up in the garage?"

My mother cocks her head and frowns. Her confusion is understandable since she mentioned those dishes over two years ago. "I guess they must still be out there somewhere. We can have a look."

Her eyes meet mine again briefly before she walks toward the kitchen. I glance at the living room as I follow her, where pictures of me and Cassie sit positioned about the same on her new mantel as they did on her old one. The living room holds the same furniture as the other house too. Neat as a pin, all of it, suggesting that she quite likely never spends any time in there. Overall, the effect is one of a shrine to the past but no one visiting here—if anyone ever does—would know that. They'd just see an orderly room in a well-kept little house. She's held on as much as possible, my mother. I have to hand it to her and it's not like I can claim having suffered more loss. I didn't. I'm down a sister, she's down a daughter. We're both down a husband. The score is even but I'm still losing by a long shot.

I'm happy to see that the kitchen is at least a little bit of a mess. Nothing like my place but a few dishes sit in the sink and a milk carton rests on the counter. The coffee machine huffs and gurgles as it finishes making a pot. Naturally, my mother offers and I accept. Coffee sounds great, actually, since I'm tired as hell and didn't think to stop at Starbucks before getting onto the highway.

My mother looks me up and down again, doing a much better job now that she's not caught by surprise. "It's great to see you. Can I get you something to eat?"

I could say no but then I'd feel ungrateful. Plus, her instincts are sound. I haven't eaten since yesterday afternoon.

My mother goes about scrambling eggs and making toast while I sip my coffee. I wonder if I should tell her about the old woman who passes through the room but, whoever she is, she doesn't seem at all concerned with us or what we're doing. One thing I've learned in a very brief time is that way more houses have ghosts than people like to imagine. What we call haunted houses are just those where the ghosts have some sort of bone to pick with those of us still here on this side. A lot of the time, ghosts hang out quietly, bothering no one as they continue to go through many of the same motions each day that they did while living. Others pass through the tunnel of light. Why, I have no idea. Life's a mystery. So is death. Big surprise.

My mother brings the plates to the table and sits across from me. She takes a breath and brightens her eyes.

"This looks great," I say.

"It's just scrambled eggs, but thank you," she says. "How are you doing, sweetie?"

Presumably, it's a rhetorical question. After all, I saw my own reflection before coming inside. "Maybe I didn't really come here for the dishes."

I catch my mother in mid-bite of her toast but she nods as she chews. She swallows and says, "I wondered."

Now that I've outed myself, I'm not entirely sure where to start. And maybe if I'd gotten some sleep, I'd pick a better place but I don't. "The fish was dead," I say.

I half-expect her to look at me strangely, like she has no idea what I'm talking about. Instead, she holds my gaze. Evidently, she hasn't forgotten either. "Well, that was such a long time ago."

"Yes, it was. But last night it happened again."

My mother shakes her head. "I don't understand."

"My cat was dead and the same thing happened. Only this time it was me. I picked him up and he came back to life. I saw him, Mom. He was dead. Cold, stiff. Dead."

My mother sets her toast down and reaches across the table to touch my hand. "Honey, how much sleep are you getting?"

I shake my head. "You've got it backwards. None of this is happening because I don't get enough sleep." I plunk my cup down too hard. "I don't get enough sleep because all of this stuff keeps happening!"

I didn't mean to raise my voice but if my own mother won't take me seriously, who the hell will? The effect, though, is that she looks a little frightened. Suddenly, I have a gut feeling about something. My mother knew something was up with Cassie. She knew and she was scared. "She was like me, wasn't she? Cassie, I mean."

My mother averts her eyes and shakes her head. She doesn't say anything.

"Did she talk to ghosts? Did you see her make a light appear in her hands like I did? What else happened? Mom, what was it?"

I stare at her until she forces herself to meet my gaze again. Her eyes fill and her hand trembles as she sets down her own mug. "Cassie could do things," she says. "She saw things. You knew it. Your father and I did too."

"But you kept acting like none of it happened. Why? I just don't get it."

"Because I wanted to protect her." Tears run down my mother's face. "I kept thinking maybe I could protect her."

Now, it's me who reaches out and takes hold of her hand. "From what, Mom? From what?"

It takes a moment before she manages to answer. "I don't know," she says, wiping her eyes. "I just had a very bad feeling about it. And I was right, wasn't I? God, I wish I was wrong but I was right. And now I have to worry about you too."

CHAPTER 8

Once she finally opened up about things, I learned a lot more from my mother than I'd ever imagined when I decided to go there. Maybe she'd been dying to talk about it for all of these years, or maybe she felt like it couldn't much matter anymore. Or maybe she thought that, by telling me, I might learn something that would protect me from whatever it was that had her so scared. That part, I can only assume boils down to something between natural parental anxiety, an understandable confusion regarding what she'd been dealing with and a certain level of twenty-twenty hindsight vision. Which doesn't mean the same fear applies going forward, I tell myself.

Still, my mother's instinct all along had been to do whatever possible to steer Cassie away from the abilities she displayed. Yes, I learned, on a number of occasions Cassie had claimed seeing people others couldn't see. It's not like I hadn't experienced that too, but what big sister is going to take her little sister seriously when she reports that she's not, in fact, mumbling to herself but is actually addressing her friend Marjorie who lived in a house sometime in the misty past where your house stood now? Not that she phrased it quite that way but my basic reaction at the time had been to nod, tune her out, and go back to blasting boyband music through my Walkman.

My mother also divulged that Cassie had sometimes predicted upcoming events. On the morning that my mother learned of her own mother's death, Cassie told her that our grandmother was with Anna again. My mother hadn't yet told us, nor did either of us know that our grandmother once had a sister named Anna. Another time, when my sister was four, she told my mother that I'd be seeing the doctors soon. Less than a week later, I came down with rotavirus and was hospitalized overnight. Why had my mother never told me any of this before? It scared the shit out of her, plain and simple. Her reaction had been denial and to hope it all just went away again.

Suddenly, the thought hits me like a ton of bricks and I stomp on the brakes too hard. Thankfully, I'm approaching a red light but there's still a screech of tires behind me. I stare at myself in the rearview mirror and say, "Holy shit."

The light changes and the car behind me honks to get me moving again. My pulse is racing and I'm somewhere between exhilarated and terrified. And confused, definitely confused. If it was just Cassie, I'm sure I could have gone on making up one reason or another why it couldn't have actually happened. And if it was just me, same deal. Fish, cat, whatever. But both of us? Could each instance have been a total coincidence? Sure, possibly. That even seems like the most logical explanation—after all, the world is also full of truly mind-blowing coincidences. But obviously there's also a fairly huge pattern here.

Cassie was displaying traits quite a bit like the traits I've been displaying only lately. Had something happened to her to initiate it? Or, for her, had it just come more naturally? It seems that, for me, I had to nearly get killed to get things rolling. Either way, there's no denying that Cassie and I have some serious woo-woo stuff in common, just not at the same time. Which leads me to wonder if my mother might have been intuitively right in thinking she had something to worry about and that something very bad was going to happen.

I glance at myself again in the rearview, where I see that I definitely don't look a whole lot better for the breakfast and coffee.

"Holy shit," I say again, but this time with a sinking feeling in my stomach. Is my mother right in being worried about me too? It doesn't seem to make sense but something deep inside tells me that I better watch my back.

~~~

After about twenty minutes of circling the block, I manage to snag street parking near VCU. I get out and make my way down to Grace Street, where I remember those two girls saying Rachel worked at a coffee shop called Percolator. The place must be new since I've never heard of it before. It's not too long before I spot it, though, on the opposite side of the street almost at the corner of Laurel. I'm almost at the door when a kid lopes by, catching my attention. There's just something about the way he walks, gazing down at the ground as if he's deep in thought. The feeling I get is that he's been going through something lately, although I have no idea why I get that feeling. It's the weirdest thing, but it's one of those times when I just know. I stop walking and turn.

"Excuse me," I say. "Are you by any chance Gary Draper?"

The kid stops and turns to face me. He stares, understandably confused. "Why?"

It's a good question. Now that I'm facing him, I'm not exactly sure where to start. *Oh, hey, I just happened to see the ghost of a girl you know*, doesn't seem like a good bet. But I have to start somewhere. "I met a friend of yours. A guy named Ed."

The kid cocks his head. "Ed Pavlos?"

Ed didn't tell me his last name but there's something about the way he says it that tells me he only knows one guy named Ed. "Right, that's the one," I say. "Do you have a minute?"

Gary glances around, not sure what to think but it's not as if I look particularly threatening. "I guess."

"Which way are you heading? I'll walk with you."

"Okay, sure."

He waits for me to catch up and we start walking back the way I just came. I nod in the direction of the coffee shop behind us. "Still working at Percolator?"

Gary hesitates. "Yeah. Not sure for how much longer, though."

"Thinking about finding something new?"

He nods. "Thinking about it."

It's one of those times when I'm not sure if I should just say what's on my mind. It could go over either way but I decide to risk it. "Because they think you're crazy?"

The kid stops and looks at me. "What did you want to talk about. Are you a reporter or something?"

I start walking again and he does too. "Nothing like that. I used to go to school here. Taking some time off right now."

"Okay," he says, which makes as much sense as any other response. After all, why am I telling him that?

"Like I said, I met your friend. He told me a little about what happened. When Rachel Joyner went missing, I mean."

"And what? Did you know her or something?"

Another reasonable question which I'm not quite sure how to answer. At the same time, given what he experienced I'm not sure he'll have a problem with it. "I sort of had a vision," I say. "On the night she went missing."

Gary's eyes search mine to see if I'm messing with him. God knows, he probably took enough shit for his account of seeing a girl suddenly vanish. "Look," he says. "I really don't need anymore–"

"I know that must sound weird but I did," I say. "It *was* weird. But strange things happen, right? I figured, if anyone might understand, it would probably be you."

"Do you have a lot of visions?"

The question surprises me since he seems so matter of fact. Then again, if you see someone suddenly vanish, you might find yourself suddenly becoming open-minded about things. "More than I'd care to," I say. "I've been curious since talking to your friend. He said you had a pretty strange experience."

He chuckles. "Yeah, you might say that."

"Do you mind telling me about it?"

Gary drops his gaze to the ground again as we continue to walk. "I'm really sick of thinking about it," he says. "I never should have said anything. For a minute there, the cops thought I might have even had something to do with it. I took a freaking lie detector test so they'd get off my ass."

"I'm sorry. It must be rough. Same at work, I bet, right?"

"Exactly. I mean, they know me. No one there thinks I did anything. They just think I freaked out about it later and made up some weird story."

"A post-traumatic stress sort of thing."

"Right," Gary says. "But that's not how it went down. I didn't like freak out when I heard the news. I freaked out when it happened."

"When what happened?"

He stops again and stares at me, his eyes peering into mine. "Look, why am I even talking to you? Who are you, anyway?"

"Someone who lost someone," I say. "My name's Autumn, by the way. Autumn Winters."

I hold out my hand and he shakes it. The kid tries not to but then laughs. Over time, I've gotten used to it.

"Seriously?"

I smile. "Yeah, I know."

"Your parents must have a good sense of humor."

I just nod. He assumes I'm too young to have been married, to be a widow. I used to be Autumn Anderson, which was extremely convenient under certain circumstances. Then I got married and became Autumn Winters, which both dropped me to the back of the line and also became readymade joke fodder. But there's no way I'm changing my name back again.

Then he remembers the first part of what I said. "Crap, I'm sorry. What happened?"

"My sister. She went missing fifteen years ago."

Gary's eyes meet mine again. "I'm really sorry."

Again, I nod. What else is there to say? And it's not like I came to find the poor kid for sympathy. I just need information. "Do you mind telling me what happened? I promise not to tell anyone. Like I said, I just got curious when I talked to your friend."

Gary slows his pace as we walk the brick path toward the heart of the Monroe Park campus. "Did something like that happen to you? I mean, with your sister?"

I keep my eyes on his. "It might have, yes. Do you mind telling me?"

He hesitates for a moment. "It was just the two of us working. The manager took off to get some stuff and it was pretty slow. We were just like hanging out, killing time before ending our shift. It goes that way sometimes, especially later in the day. Rachel was wiping down the tables and I was behind the counter, sort of watching her."

His face colors a little when he says it and I get it. Rachel was a pretty girl and he was checking her out when she didn't think he was looking. "Then what happened?"

He shakes his head. "That's just it. Nothing. One minute she was there and the next she was just gone. I swear. There was just this one weird moment when my eyes went funny. I can't really explain it. Just this flickering sort of thing." Gary shakes his head again, his eyes wider now as he relives the experience. "And that was it. She was just gone."

I try to ignore my pounding heart. "What did you do?"

Gary nods. "Exactly, right? That's what the cops kept asking me. Nothing. I had no idea what to think. I mean, I called out for her, thinking maybe she went into the back or something. My brain said I saw what I saw but, at the same time, I didn't really see anything. I didn't know what to think. I checked out back, and then figured maybe she went into the ladies room or something. I kept waiting and kind of talked myself into thinking I must be crazy and that she just took off for some reason."

"So, you didn't tell anyone?"

He shrugs. "There was no one to tell. When Jan got back—sorry, she's the manager—she asked me where Rachel was and I told her I had no idea. But then, later I saw that thing on the news about her going missing. That's when I started telling people."

"The next day," I say.

"Yeah, that's when I heard she'd gone missing. Rachel was a commuter student so her parents must have been freaking out. She told me she had a really tight family."

It makes sense to me now how it must have seemed suspicious that Gary mentioned what happened only after the fact. But it wasn't like anyone was going to believe him, either way. I know this all too well.

I keep my eyes on his. "Listen, you're not nuts, okay? I mean, what happened to me was just like what you experienced. I was looking at my sister one minute, something strange happened with my eyes, and then she was gone."

"Holy shit," Gary says.

"Yeah, exactly. As you can imagine, no one really believed me. They thought it was trauma, that I was making it up to deal with the guilt. She was my little sister. I was supposed to be watching her."

He looks off across the campus, at all those other kids coming and going, backpacks slung across their shoulders. It's beyond strange to think that at any second one of them could just blip off the face of the planet—literally right in front of someone—while no one would have any idea where they went.

"I should probably get going," Gary says.

I nod. "Sure. Of course. Thanks for talking to me."

Gary sets off and I walk the brick path back toward my car alongside the flow of students coming and going from their classes. I reach the street and spot the ticket on my windshield. "Shit," I mutter, not really caring if anyone hears me. Did I even think about paying the meter? Looking back, I'm pretty sure I spaced that part entirely. If there were awards for being distracted, I'd be a hall of famer at this point.

Still, I'm not so distracted that, when I pull away from the curb, I fail to notice the man in my rearview mirror. He stands watching from where the brick path meets the sidewalk. As if sensing that I noticed him, he turns and follows the sidewalk in the opposite direction. I only saw him for a second, but I have no doubt that it's the same man I saw at Rory's the other night.

~~~

When I see who's calling, I consider letting it go to voicemail. I know Zach means well, that he's the kind of guy who puts others' feelings ahead of his own. He's there for me, I know, as he has been all along. After the accident, he used to call frequently. To see how I was holding up or if he could do anything, prioritizing my needs even though he'd lost his brother. And the thing was, I wasn't holding up well and I really did need help. At the same time, Zach resembles Justin way too much, in both his mannerisms and appearance. It's hard to be around him without feeling like my heart just got ripped out of my chest again. So, I kept telling him I was fine and kept my distance.

Now, of course, I know exactly why he's calling. We're coming up on a year since it happened, something I've been trying not to think about. I just can't bear the thought of that becoming our new anniversary. I sit on the sofa staring as my phone continues to rattle against the coffee table. At the last moment, I snatch it up.

"I've been meaning to call," Zach says. "You know, just to check in. How are things?"

"Doing good," I say. "How about you?" I do my best to brighten my voice, thankful that he can't see me. I can't imagine that I look any less crappy than I did eight hours ago.

"I'm good," Zach says. "Keeping busy."

It's not lost on me that Zach doesn't say "we're good." It reflects his sensitive nature that he doesn't immediately reference Ellen, his wife, or Zelda and Ethan, their two beautiful children. Zach is four years older than Justin. By the time we got married, he and Ellen already had Zelda, while Ethan was a bump in Ellen's tummy that drew nearly as much attention at our wedding as Justin and I did. Not that I resented it then, or ever have since. You'd have to be deranged not to both like and admire Ellen, a veterinarian who volunteers at an animal shelter on the weekends while raising two small children. She's just a really nice person.

"Me too," I say. "I had lunch with Molly yesterday and went to see my mother today." There, see? I really don't spend all my time drinking alone.

"How's your mother doing? Did she ever call my friend about getting her roof repaired?"

The good daughter that I am, I had no idea that my mother's roof needed repair. She could be sleeping with buckets next to her bed and I wouldn't notice. "I think so, " I say. "She mentioned something about that a while ago."

A moment of silence passes, making me wonder if Zach's referral might not have happened all that long ago. Still, all he says is, "Good. Tell her not to hesitate if she ever needs something fixed."

The topic of home repairs inspires a little improvisation, a white lie to assure Zach that I'm doing okay. "By the way, I'm painting my living room," I find myself saying. "I'm thinking the bedroom's next."

The only truth in my statement is that I considered painting my apartment. Over a year ago. The idea is to sound productive, but I wince as soon as I make the claim since now I pretty much have to paint my apartment. I can't entirely rule out Zach and Ellen dropping by sometime. Thinking that through for like three seconds before opening my mouth would have been a good idea.

"Hey, I could help with that," Zach says.

I glance up at the ceiling, where some sort of stain— mildew or water damage—spreads from the corner. Great. Now I get to paint the freaking ceiling too. "That's really nice of you," I say. "But I was thinking a project would be good. Keep me busy. How about I call you for advice?"

"Fair enough. I'll even waive my consultation fee."

I hear the smile in Zach's voice. So, that part's good. "Well, since you offered, how important is primer?" Thankfully, Zach can't see that I've flipped my laptop open and Googled interior painting, where it's strongly advised not to skip the primer.

"Really important," Zach says. "You used it in the living room, right?"

"Sure, of course."

"Okay, good. By the way, Z and E loved their birthday gifts. Z can't go anywhere without that giraffe and we can hardly get E out of those dinosaur-feet slippers."

My eyes go moist at the fact that I've never seen either gift and didn't send them. Obviously, my mother covered for me. On top of which, what kind of aunt would send gifts rather than drive a few miles? Not to mention that Zach, Ellen and the kids also moved into a new house a couple of months ago and I haven't yet gone by. Maybe the real reason I hesitated taking the call is because I'm such a loser.

We spend a few more minutes chatting but soon the call winds down, although not before Zach once again invites me to come over sometime. He's kept trying and I've kept avoiding it. In that moment, though, it finally seems like enough is enough. It's been a year. It's time for me to stop feeling sorry for myself and get some sort of life again. To at least start taking some steps in that direction. For example, spending a night with my niece and nephew rather than hunched over the bar at Rory's.

I know it's just my imagination since I've never once felt that Justin remains here. He's gone. I know that. And I'm glad about that—I wouldn't want his ghost lingering here for me or for any other reason. All the same, in that moment I feel him next to me. I imagine him smiling. *What do you think, babe?*

"You know, that sounds great," I tell Zach. "I'd really like that."

~~~

In the middle of the night, I open my eyes to the darkness. At first, I think it must be my imagination, the softly lit orb floating in the corner of my ceiling. Briefly, I wonder if it's a lingering remnant of a dream, but I watch as the light slowly descends toward me. I think of Cassie all those years ago and I do as I remember her doing. I hold out my cupped palms. In my half-awake state, I hardly think about it. I act on an instinct that feels as if it's lain dormant within me. The orb floats closer and I stare, eyes widening, as it drifts down and comes to rest in my hands. It remains there for just a moment, casting a glow across the room, before winking out.

CHAPTER 9

It isn't hard getting Rachel Joyner's address. In fact, it takes only a few minutes of searching. Her parents' names have been all over the news and their address is public information for the world to see. For the second time in two days, I find myself driving and my hands are no less clammy than before, my heart steadily pounding away. Add to that, I don't know quite why I'm going there. Well, other than the fact that it feels like some sort of window has opened within me—a window both into the past and future—and I keep thinking that whatever happened to Rachel Joyner will help me understand what's going on. That, just maybe, it will help me understand what happened to Cassie.

I cruise through a quiet suburban street, mine the only car crawling past giant homes with stone facades and multiple peaks at their rooflines. These houses must have cost a fortune. I feel no less bad for the Joyners knowing that, if they're not necessarily wealthy, clearly they're pretty well off. This is not a neighborhood where many are likely to be experiencing financial concerns.

My phone's GPS tells me that I'm close to my destination and I half-expect to see news trucks lining the curb. Most likely, just days ago, the media vultures were camped out hoping for possible interviews and news fodder about the missing girl. Apparently, enough time has passed that they've moved on. Rachel's name and face are no longer front page news. No one has to say it since it's assumed. She's a lost cause. The clock ticks quietly in the background, counting down the hours until she turns up dead.

The GPS identifies a house essentially identical to the others, the only difference being the shade of siding chosen, the planters on the front porch and the color of the decorative flag flapping in the breeze. The flag shows fall leaves, a festive splash of color that now seems out of place. I feel like I'm trespassing, that I have no right to be here. All the same, I slow to a crawl and then park not quite in front of the property.

Since the accident, ghosts have continued to somehow find me. Never once, though, have I reached out. Now, I've come to the only logical place I can think of.

After all, Rachel has to be somewhere and her home seems a likely choice. I close my eyes and breathe deeply, deliberately slowing my pulse. I picture Rachel's face. Not the one I've seen on the news but the girl who came to me asking for help. I speak to her within my mind.

Rachel, are you here somewhere? I'm sorry about the other night. Will you still talk to me?

My eyes fly open as someone raps against the passenger side window. A woman looks in at me. She's in her late fifties, maybe early sixties. Not a speck of gray hair on her head, not in a neighborhood like this. She holds a leash in one hand, the other poised to rap again. A dog I can't see pulls against her arm.

"Are you okay?"

Her voice comes muffled through the glass. I think about driving off but I roll the window down.

"I saw you sitting here," she says. "I wondered if something might be wrong."

"I had a migraine," I say. "I decided to pull over."

She nods like she understands but her brow creases. "Should you be driving?"

"I'm okay now. I'm fine. Thank you."

"Are you sure?"

I nod and do my best to smile.

The woman hesitates, possibly sensing that I'm lying. Still, she has no reason to question me. Her arm quirks as her dog pulls again. She walks off and I glance into my rearview mirror to be sure she keeps moving. I close my eyes again. *I'm trying to help you. I'm trying to find out what happened. Can you hear me?*

I open my eyes and look at the house. A few moment pass before the front door opens. A man appears first, then a woman, both glaring out at me. They exhibit both anger and fear. They hold themselves framed in the doorway as if they're trapped inside. I can't meet their eyes. I've come here with no plan, no way to explain why I've chosen to intrude on their pain. My motivations may be different but, to that agonized middle-aged couple, I'm just another form of vulture. I start the car and put it into drive. I roll forward, afraid to glance back, but something tells me that I should. When I do, I see Rachel watching me from the upstairs window.

~~~

I tell myself that the buckets of primer and paint I haul into my apartment speak to the fact that I'm starting to do better. My plan for tomorrow is to get up early, to start on the bedroom first. I should be able to manage that without too much inconvenience since, half the time, I sleep on the sofa anyway. I make myself a salad and sauté a chicken breast. I watch TV and think about calling Molly.

But what would I tell her? *Hey, guess what? I'm thinking about re-enrolling at school? You know, start getting out into the world a little more. Oh, I also went looking for a ghost today. That's right, I went by her house.*

I'm sure that's exactly the kind of thing an expectant mother wants to hear from her best friend. I check the fridge later with a sinking feeling to confirm that I actually, for once, forgot to buy both beer and wine. I go back into the living room telling myself that I need neither, that my can of Diet Pepsi will do the trick perfectly, that I'm tired anyway. About ten minutes later I'm catching the bus to Rory's.

~~~

I was hoping to see Penny but Tim is tending bar tonight. Not that Tim's a bad guy. It's just that sometimes he can be a little full of himself. He's a bass player working in a few bands, one of which has actually been getting some local airplay. Or so he's told me. Not that I would know since I almost never listen to the radio. All the same, good for him. I hope he becomes a rock star someday.

"Hey Autumn," he says, as I slide onto one of the barstools. "How's tricks?"

That's another thing about Tim. He's a few years younger than me but likes using outdated expressions. But who am I to judge? Maybe he's close to his grandmother.

"Tricks are good," I say, since I'm not sure how else to respond.

"Let me guess," Tim says. "You have a hankering for beer tonight."

"Beer is what I'm hankering," I say.

True, it's a fifty-fifty shot but Tim actually is good at guessing whether I'm in a beer or wine mood. And he never hits on me, despite the fact that I'm always alone. I could take that as an insult, but I've chosen to interpret it as respect. All in all, Tim does have his qualities as a bartender.

I manage to pass an hour nursing just the one beer, spending the time trying not to think about ghosts, vanishing people, dead cats jumping back to life or other strange phenomenon. I came here to stop thinking about those things. Still, I keep seeing the lost look in Rachel's eyes as she stared out at me from that window. I just don't know how to help her. Can anyone help her or will she remain trapped between this world and the next? I don't know, just as I don't know why I was suddenly cursed with being able to see people like her. The fact is, I just want something approximating normal, even if just for an hour or so. For me these days, Rory's is as close as I can get.

By the time I finally cave and decide to order another beer, Tim is talking to a guy I've seen in here from time to time. I forget his name, but Tim mentioned before that he works some sort of tech job for one of the news stations. Audio-visual stuff, I think. Either an editor or cameraman. Eventually, that guy sets off and Tim remembers I'm still at the bar. I flag him down for another beer.

"Took you long enough," Tim says. "I was getting worried about you."

I try not to take it personally but, obviously, it doesn't reflect well on me that not drinking fast enough is noticeably out of character. "Glad I didn't let you down." I squeeze in some lime. "But it's going to be just the two tonight."

Understandably, Tim has his doubts. "Just let me know," he says, as if I didn't just do exactly that.

Fair enough, I think. I hardly believe it myself.

Tim gestures to the recently vacated spot at the bar. "Did you hear what Caleb was saying? Kind of weird."

I'm afraid to ask since the last thing I need is more weirdness in my life. Still, I ask. "What's up?"

Tim gives the bar top a quick wipe with a towel. "Something he heard about at the news station. I guess they found a body the other day."

My heart leaps in my chest. "Was it Rachel Joyner?"

Tim draws a blank at the name. He stares at me for a moment before making the connection. "That girl who went missing? No, not her. Some lady. In her thirties, I think. They found her out by the Diamond."

"That's really sad." My pulse slows again and I can't help but feel relieved. Of course, I don't want to hear that Rachel is dead. At the same time, strangely there'd be comfort in knowing I'd simply encountered another ghost.

"Yeah, definitely," Tim says. "According to Caleb, it looked to be a suicide."

I take another sip of my beer, suddenly remembering where we started. "Sadly, I'm not sure how weird any of that is."

Tim nods. "Right. I forgot the weird part. Caleb said the cops had no idea who she was. No ID, nothing like that. But they put stuff out there and something came up positive. Turns out she went missing like twenty years ago."

I check his eyes but I can tell he doesn't know. The only person I've ever told at Rory's is Penny. She wouldn't have told anyone when I asked her not to. "Missing," is all I can manage.

"In like Ohio or someplace like that. Can you believe that shit? It's like she disappeared back in time and then washed up here two decades later."

I drain the rest of my beer and slide the bottle toward him without saying anything.

"Wow, that was fast," Tim says. "Guess you must be feeling better."

~~~

I stand at the bus stop, thinking all I have to do is get home. After that, I'm never coming out again. Maybe I'll paint the place and maybe I won't. Either way, it won't matter because no one will ever see me again except Louie. I'll just hide away with my resurrected one-eyed cat until I either grow old and die or finish losing my mind. Either seems fine with me at the moment. As long as I don't have to think about ghosts, or ghosts who don't think they're ghosts, or why some people cross over to the other side while others get kicked back again.

Keep it together, Autumn, I think. Remember the new plan. Keep taking baby steps until you have some sort of a shot at a normal life again.

As if to make a mockery of that very thought, I suddenly realize he's there again. Somehow, I feel him beside me, an expectant presence. Please, no. Not now. Please.

"They say it's supposed to snow tonight."

I tell myself not to engage, to just ignore him as I've attempted in the past. At the same time, I'm not in the mood for taking any more shit from whatever realm I tapped into on the day I should have died. I turn to look at him. Just as before, he wears a heavy coat and blows on his hands. "It's only September," I say.

"I knew you could hear me."

I keep my eyes on his. "Yes, I can hear you. You know that you died, right?"

He cocks his head as if I just spoke a different language. "They say we might even have a white—"

"Do you even know how long it's been?" I feel the current start to pulse through me. Just faintly but it's becoming familiar, that tingling of my skin.

"You wore those earrings last time, the long silver ones. I liked the way they—"

"Are you afraid? Is that it?"

He shakes his head. "I can't remember the last time it was this cold."

Suddenly, the images rush back at me again. Him driving the truck through the snow, in a different time, a different place. It's night and the snow falls heavily as he travels, his vehicle the only one on the road. He keeps checking his rearview mirror.

"They say there hasn't been a white Christmas around here since 1969."

The truck stops on a bridge. He gets out. Below, the river churns and roils, foam glistening white in the moonlight.

Another image shoots into my mind and, along with it, a feeling. No, not a feeling. A certainty. "Was that when you did it? Is that why you came here, to get away from the snow?"

He turns and glances down the street as if waiting for the bus to arrive. "Sure is cold out tonight," he says.

He throws a tarp back and looks around one more time to be sure. He lifts the body from the back of the truck. She's small, whoever she was. It takes him almost no effort to lift her.

"Look at me," I say. "Snow makes you think about that night, doesn't it?"

He shakes his head and blows on his hands.

"Who was she? Did they ever find her?" They did, I know. It's him they never found. I see him wandering these streets, jobless and destitute, drinking the years away as he fades like a ghost long before dying. "How long did you live after that? Twenty years? Thirty? How many?"

Suddenly, his face crumples and his eyes scrunch closed. He bends forward, his hands clasped as if in prayer. He speaks softly as tears start to fall, his voice a jagged whisper. "I don't know. I wanted it to end but it just kept going."

"Why did you do it?"

He pivots toward me again, his face a mask of pain. "I didn't mean for it to happen. I loved her but she didn't love me. It just happened—you have to believe me!"

The charge keeps building inside me, spreading out from my solar plexus. The current courses through my veins and down my arms.

"Please say you believe me." He gasps for air as tears run down his cheeks. "Please!"

I stare into his eyes and see the terror there. A terror different from hers, whoever she was, one that lasted much longer. Each day of his life, through all of the decades after he did it, consisted of a hellish terror lasting an eternity. Then decades past when it should have ended, it still kept going. He's been punished a million times over and I can't say if this is when it stops. That part isn't up to me. But somehow I know this—I can end it here. I don't know why, or what it means, but I can. I raise my cupped palms and a glowing sphere rests within them, its light continuing to spread outward. Despite the repugnance I felt before at what I saw, I bring my eyes to his again. He watches the light in my hands and I see that somehow he knows what it means.

"I believe you," I say.

I thrust out my hands and a burst of light leaps toward him. He stumbles back as it engulfs him like a closing tunnel. A moment later, he's gone.

CHAPTER 10

I stand at the bus stop alone. At least, that's what I think until I look across the street. He stands there, staring back. This time, I don't give him time to skulk off again or try to convince myself that it's some sort of coincidence. It's not. I may not know what the hell is going on but that much I know.

I charge straight at him, crossing the street without bothering to look. A car swerves past, just missing me, but I keep my eyes locked on his. He holds his ground, waiting for me to approach.

"Who the hell are you?" My breath comes in short gasps, partly from my dash across the road, but mostly from the adrenalin rush of what just happened.

"I didn't mean to scare you," he says.

"Scare me?" My arms dangle tensed at my sides, still buzzing as if I touched a live wire. "Don't fucking flatter yourself. Who are you?"

His eyes meet mine beneath the streetlight. "My name's Ian Bloom."

"You've been following me." I half-expect him to deny it but he doesn't.

"Yes. I follow people. That's what I do."

"What kind of creepy shit is that?" I fight to keep my voice steady, but one hand has itself wrapped around the can of pepper spray in my purse. I'm this close to blasting the thing at his face when he speaks again.

"I'm a private investigator. But, sure, it can get a little creepy. Kind of goes with the territory sometimes."

"What the hell are you talking about? Who hired you, the insurance company? Is that what this is? Because I can assure you that my husband is officially dead. No one scammed any life policy cash off of you assholes, if that's what you're thinking the deal is."

He shakes his head, a trace of sadness in his eyes. "No one hired me."

"But you just said—"

"I know. I've been following you for other reasons. Case-related, maybe. Probably, in fact. But not because anyone asked me to."

The last thing I need is another goddamned riddle in my life. I'm still shaking when I point the pepper spray at his face.

He steps back. "Whoa. Take it easy."

"Elaborate. Now."

"Can you please lower that thing. That stuff hurts."

"That's the idea, asshole." But something about the way he says it—the measured calm, the simple honesty—makes me lower the can of spray. Suddenly, it occurs to me to ask. "What did you just see?"

He gestures toward the bus stop. "I saw you throw what looked like a ball of light at a ghost. I think. I don't know. Whatever that was, well, let's just say it's beyond the scope of my experience. Did he ask you to cross him? Is that what happened?"

I come up short for two reasons. First, because, if I heard correctly, he just admitted seeing me talk to a ghost. That's never happened before. Second, because I'm not sure what he means by the question.

Ian seems to understand because he tries again. "That's what happened, right? You helped him cross. I've never seen anything like it before."

His meaning sinks in. "Not exactly. But you could see him?"

He nods, and there's a weariness to his gesture that speaks volumes to me. "Yes, I saw him. I've seen him before at that same spot."

My pulse starts to slow as my breathing evens out. Only now do I think of stepping up onto the curb. I hadn't even realized, but I've been standing in the street the entire time. "How often does it happen? Seeing ghosts. That's what you're saying right?"

"A little too often, although they don't seem to notice me. You, on the other hand, seem to be in something of a different league. You're sure he didn't ask you to cross him?"

"By cross him, I guess you mean send him to the other side."

"That's what they call it," Ian says. "As in, helping someone leave this plane of existence. Typically, they have to agree to accepting your help."

I shake my head, the images coming back to me—the truck on the bridge, the girl's body, the haunted terror in that man's eyes at the things he'd had to live with. "I'm pretty sure I made that decision."

"I've never heard of it working that way."

I slip the pepper spray back into my bag, not ready to consider the implications of what he just said. There must be some sort of mistake, or maybe he doesn't know what he's talking about. "How long have you been following me?"

"Since I found out about what happened to your sister," he says.

CHAPTER 11

It's probably not the smartest thing, but I follow Ian to his car and let him drive us across town. I'm in a daze from the overall kaleidoscope of shit that's been coming at me, but what Ian just said served as basically the knockout punch. As he drives, it occurs to me that might be exactly what a serial rapist and killer would want, to use his wiles to manipulate to a point where you're under his spell and completely vulnerable. I realize this. Still, I go with him. Maybe it's the kindness of his eyes or his gentle mannerism, or maybe it's that sense of shared burden that he communicated to me before—but something tells me that I can trust him. If nothing else lately, I've started listening to my instincts.

He parks in front of a place I've driven past but never been into before. A diner that I always figured for retro-trendy, but which turns out to look like it's been hanging in there since before either of us was born. It's quiet with just a handful of people at the counter and a few occupied booths. Music flows into the room from the bar in back where more people sit hunched over drinks.

We take one of the booths and it's not long before a middle-aged waitress arrives. I order a glass of wine and Ian asks for tea.

"Irish or English?"

"I'm sorry. English tonight," Ian says. "Thanks, Brenda."

Their familiarity finally allows my nerves to settle back into place—the current, that buzzing feeling, finally fading. "Is this where you come to...drink tea?"

"When I stay in town," Ian says. "My office isn't far from here. I thought this might be better than Rory's, since that's where you go to relax."

"Which you know because you've been stalking me."

He winces but smiles. "I'm sorry, but, yes. In a manner of speaking anyway."

"And now you're going to explain."

Ian keeps his eyes on mine. "I'll do my best. I'm not sure how much you'll believe."

"Try me."

I'm doing my best to remain cold but, the fact is, he has a nice face. Thick, curly dark hair and big brown eyes that don't seem to hide much. Part of me wonders if he might have chosen the wrong line of work since he seems kind of easy to read. Then again, having a trustworthy face might give him a natural advantage when digging around for information.

"Let me ask you this," Ian says. "What's your view on coincidence versus fate?"

The waitress drops off our drinks and I wait until she's gone. "Did we come here for a philosophical conversation?"

"Fair enough. Let's circle back to that later. I'll try to start at the beginning."

I take a sip of my wine. "That's where stories usually start."

He nods. "True, but this story has more than one beginning. Like I said, coincidences. Maybe. Part of it starts when I was going to college in Charlottesville."

"UVA?" I ask, just to be sure.

Ian adds a little milk to his tea. "Right. I went there for a couple of years, although that's not where I finished. Anyway, I was happy there. I made some friends and then ended up meeting Shannon."

Maybe it's the look in his eyes or maybe it's his tone, but something tells me this part of the story doesn't have a happy ending. "Girlfriend?"

He sighs. "For about a year. We were pretty crazy about each other, basically inseparable from day one. We were young but I was already thinking about her being the one. You know, maybe getting married someday. Kids, possibly, down the road. All of that. I'd never felt like that about anyone before." He glances down at the table, then his eyes meet mine again. "Then she went missing."

A chill runs up my spine and I try not to shiver. As has been happening more and more lately, I know before I ask. Still, I ask. "Was she ever found?"

He shakes his head.

My heart starts beating faster. "What happened?"

"No one really knows," Ian says. "One night, she went out with her friends. They got some dinner, went to a party. They decided to head back to campus later and went to catch a bus. Suddenly, Shannon just wasn't with them anymore." He shrugs and keeps his eyes on mine. "Just like that, gone."

I shake my head, not willing to believe what he's telling me. It feels like the walls are closing in, and I reach for my wine glass.

Ian nods as if he knows what I'm experiencing. "No one really believed them," he says. "They'd been drinking, after all. The police did breathalyzers, questioned each of them separately. The whole deal. I don't think they suspected foul play, but they couldn't exactly rule it out either. After all, their story made no sense. No one just vanishes while they're walking down the street with their friends. Something had to have happened that they just weren't talking about, even if it was just that they hooked up with the wrong guys or something like that."

When I speak, my voice comes out little more than a whisper. "But nothing like that happened."

"Right, nothing like that happened. Shannon's friends all stuck to their story. The other strange thing about their account was that all of them said something about the light getting funny. Some said maybe it was the streetlights flickering, others said they weren't sure, that they just sort of remembered seeing pulsing lights. Nothing consciously remembered. A detail that they probably wouldn't have even thought about if they hadn't been forced to search their memory. Possibly. Who can say? But what they all remembered was suddenly realizing Shannon wasn't with them, almost like they'd just blacked out for a moment."

"How do I know you're not lying to me?" Even as I say it, I know he's not. Not one part of me thinks he's lying.

"Her last name was Meyers. She was from Alexandria. I won't be offended if you want to Google her name. Her case comes right up."

I reach for my phone, but then change my mind. "What happened after that?"

Ian shrugs. "Nothing. Shannon was gone and I had to deal with it. Not exactly the best time in my life. The next few years were rough, but they were also years where I had to accept something about myself that I'd been unwilling to face. I guess this would be as good a time as any to ask. Do you believe in psychics?"

I check his eyes to see if he's kidding. "You're talking to a woman who sees ghosts."

Ian shrugs. "True. I guess that would have to leave you somewhat open-minded. But how long have you believed in them?"

I think about that for a moment and the fact is, not very long. Not long ago they belonged to the realm of movies and television shows I never bothered to watch. Or internet scams set up for the lost, lonely and desperate.

Ian interprets my silence correctly. "Right, exactly," he says. "Neither did I at one time. But, looking back, I realize that I always got feelings about things. Basically, I did my best to ignore the whole deal since it gave me the creeps. But after Shannon disappeared, it really started kicking in for me. That was probably the worst time in my life. Let's just say I took certain measures to block out what was coming at me."

I glance at Ian's mug of tea and realize what he's telling me. He spent some time trying to drink his way into denial too.

"But sometimes the door opens whether you want it to or not," Ian says. "For me, that was in Iraq. We were on patrol, just about to knock on a door, and suddenly I hear a voice telling me to stop right now, to back off. I had maybe three seconds to listen or not. I decided to listen. I tried telling the other guys with me, but I was the only one who heard the voice. After the blast, I was also the only one still standing. From there, I pretty much couldn't ignore that voice anymore."

The waitress comes by and asks us if we'd like anything. Ian waits, letting me decide. I decide I'm fine with the one glass of wine. I also decide to stay and hear the rest of what Ian has to say.

Ian checks my eyes, then continues. "Fast forward a few years. I come back to Richmond and decide to become a cop. I put in a few years. I finish my degree at night and online. I take a test, I interview, and, before you know it, I find myself a rookie detective occasionally working on missing person cases. Some of those cases remain unsolved but just a few still nag at people because they're so peculiar."

Ian makes eye contact to make sure I follow his meaning, which I do.

"Cassie," I say.

"Exactly. It's one of those puzzling mysteries that just bug the shit out of cops. Two girls at the park and suddenly one of them is gone. Poof. These guys can get pretty jaded, but a story like that? Shit, it could have been one of their daughters. It just sticks, keeps getting talked about over the years. You can also guess why it resonated with me. But the one thing I felt pretty sure I saw—the one thing that, of course, the other guys couldn't see—was a pattern. These guys are all about patterns, but not one of them is going to give three seconds to a pattern that, well, for lack of a better word, suggests something supernatural."

I don't know why, but it's only when Ian says it that the implication becomes clear. With as many strange things that have happened, I kept looking for a logical answer, something that fits in with the real world. Or what we think of as the real world. Suddenly, just like a door opened for him, one opens for me. But the truth, I realize, is that the door was always open and I'm only just now starting to accept it.

"Supernatural," I say. "That's what this is about, isn't it?"

"I don't see what else it could possibly be," Ian says. "It sure as hell isn't normal. Just like anything, once you become aware of it, you can't exactly forget it again. Once I found out about the similarities between what happened to your sister and what Shannon's friends said happened, I couldn't stop thinking about it. I'd never stopped thinking about her—not for a day—and then I find out the same thing happened. Two cases doesn't make for a pattern, though. Two cases is just coincidence. Then I learned about a couple of other similar cases. After that, I became somewhat obsessed. A little too obsessed to focus properly on burglaries and drug dealing, which didn't exactly go unnoticed. So, for that and a few other reasons, I decided to become a private investigator."

"Is that when you started following me?"

"As well as to investigate the other cases. Originally, I'd planned on talking to you. But that was right when you and your husband were in the car accident. I'm sorry for your loss, by the way. I'm sure it hasn't been easy."

Understatement of the year, I think. But I just say, "Thank you."

Ian keeps his eyes on mine. He understands, of course. What else is there for either of us to say about that?

"Eventually, you got out of the hospital and started frequenting Rory's." He looks away, as if not to embarrass me with the fact that he's probably seen me in there getting hammered alone a thousand times. "So, I decided I'd drop by every so often too. Just in case."

"What were you even looking for? My sister's been gone fifteen years. I don't understand."

Ian shrugs. "At first, you were the only lead I had. Call it instinct, intuition, whatever you like, but something told me that you were going to help me figure out what the hell

94

is going on. And, if what I saw tonight was any indication, I'd say I was right."

I'm not sure if I should say anything. I don't know him. But the desire to confide in someone wins out. "You might say that."

"Then, last week, I saw her come into the bar and try talking to you."

"You mean Rachel Joyner."

"I didn't find out her name until the next day, but, yes. Do you mind telling me what you two talked about?"

I hesitate, once again thinking that it can't possibly be true, but Ian keeps his eyes on mine as he waits. "She told me she's not dead," I say. "She said someone took her body."

I expect surprise, disbelief. Ian exhibits neither. "I suspect she's telling the truth," he says.

"That's not possible." Even as I say it, I know it's not because I don't believe what Rachel Joyner told me. It's that I don't want to believe it. Not if it means what I think it means.

"Which brings us back to the other cases I mentioned," Ian says. "Emily Richards and Ryan McKenzie. Same deal. Each of them suddenly went missing. Both times, witnesses offered similar accounts. There one minute, gone the next."

"What happened when you investigated?"

"In Ryan McKenzie's case, I only got so far before hitting a dead end. Emily Richards, on the other hand, I managed to find."

My heart starts beating fast again. "Dead?"

"Alive, but it didn't stay that way for long. She insisted that I'd mixed her up with someone else and told me to take a hike. And it wasn't like I could do anything about it."

"Did you tell anyone that you'd seen her?"

Ian nods. "Sure. Not that it mattered. The next day, she was found floating in the James River. She'd been missing for over a year and suddenly there she was."

I stare at him, as if through tunnel vision. If what he's saying is true, it means Cassie could still be alive. Has been this entire time. No, it's insane, all of it. He must be deranged, and I don't know why I'm sitting here listening to him. More likely, I'm psychotic and he's just another hallucination. One more among many.

I shake my head. "None of it makes any sense. Like you said, they're all just coincidences. What happened to your girlfriend, my sister, the others. There's nothing connecting them."

"I've thought about that," Ian says. "A lot. Sometimes coincidences are just coincidences, nothing more. Other times, though, they seem more like a message being delivered to a specific recipient."

Ian takes another sip of his tea, and the feeling I get is that he wants to be sure I'm paying attention.

He continues. "Although I'm the one who noticed the coincidences, something tells me I'm just helping deliver the message. The fact is, I think the message is intended for someone who can take action on the information."

His eyes remain on mine.

"I take it, you mean me."

Ian nods, his gaze serious. "That's exactly what I mean."

I look at the hallucination sitting across from me. "I need to go home," I say. "I really need to go home."

~~~

Half an hour later, I'm home. Thankfully, Louie has shown signs of life by devouring his food and has left no gifts for me tonight in return. They say cats are selfish and this is one of those times I fully appreciate the lack of an offering. I open the fridge and realize that, once again, I forgot to buy beer. I'm not sure I like this. The new me isn't turning out exactly as intended. I think I prefer blackout drunk to woman who can vaporize guilty ghosts. Yes, I need to be alone. I crawl into bed and fall asleep much faster than I imagined possible. But it's been a very long day. Unfortunately, it doesn't feel long at all before I wake up again and realize that I'm no longer alone.

CHAPTER 12

"Can you see me?"

She stands in my bedroom doorway, flickering in the darkness as if struggling to manifest. I've seen this before, how sometimes ghosts appear translucent while others can appear nearly physical. Why, I'm not sure. It might have something to do with how long they've been stuck and how committed they are to remaining here. But those are ghosts, and my conversation with Ian leaves me uncertain about what I'm seeing now.

"Yes, I can see you." I sit up and swing my legs over the side of my bed.

Rachel's eyes shine moist as they look into mine. "And you can hear me, right?"

I nod. "Yes."

"It's you, right? I saw you at that bar. The other night when I..." She shakes her head, not sure how to finish the sentence. "You came to my house. I saw you. Why did you come there?"

I think back to this morning, and it feels like years ago. "I don't know. I just... I keep thinking about you. About what you told me."

She steps toward me, becoming less translucent as she approaches. "You didn't believe me before."

"I'm sorry."

"I need you to believe me. You're the only one who's been able see me." Her hands tremble as she reaches out, pleading. "Please!"

I make myself say the words, afraid of the door I'm opening. "You said they took your body. I don't understand. Who? How is that possible?"

Tears start running down her cheeks. "I was at work and they came in. They said I was coming with them, that I'd been chosen. They laughed, like it was some kind of joke. They thought it was funny!"

She begins to flicker again, as if something keeps trying to pull her away.

"I understand it's painful," I say. "Try to hang on. I need you to tell me what happened. Can you do that?"

She brings her eyes to mine again, and I realize how young she is. Or, was. I'm not sure what to think. She takes a breath to collect herself and, once again, I wonder why we exhibit these physical displays of emotion when we're no longer physical—that we cry and gasp and tremble.

"It was just me and Gary," Rachel says. "We thought they were customers. They started talking to us."

"How many of them were there? What did they look like?"

"Three. Two guys. They were young, probably in their twenties. And her. She was older."

"How old?"

"In her thirties, I guess. She had a tattoo on her arm. I remember that. Some sort of symbols, I think."

Rachel's flickering has slowed but not stopped and I remind myself to tread carefully. The feeling I get is that she could be gone just as quickly as she appeared. "Then what happened?"

"They started talking about me like I wasn't even there. They didn't care!"

My eyes start to well at her confusion and suffering. "What did they say?"

"That they'd noticed me, they'd seen me running. One of the guys reached out and touched me. He looked at the woman and said, 'Just like I told you. She's in great shape.' I had this horrible feeling. I felt sick, like I was about to be raped! I went to slap him and that's when it happened." Rachel shudders and flickers away, one moment standing beside me and then back near the doorway again.

"Rachel, what happened? You came here to tell me."

"My eyes, they went funny. It was like everything suddenly went out of focus. I saw lights. "

A chill runs up my spine, my pulse escalating. I try to keep my voice steady. "Then what happened?"

"I don't know. I don't really remember. Suddenly, I was in their car, then out by the stadium. I don't want to talk about it!"

She's in the hall now and I jump off the bed. I run into the hallway as she keeps flickering away. "Rachel, please. You came here to tell me!"

"That's where they left her body," she says. "That's when they took me!"

A moment later, I stand in the hallway staring at empty space. Part of me wants to think of that presence as having been a ghost—every experience I've had so far tells me it was—while a deeper part of me knows it wasn't. And it scares the living hell out of me.

CHAPTER 13

They'd gathered in Paul's dining room to talk beneath the glow of the chandelier, before them an expanse of food ranging from blocks of cheese and bowls of nuts to colorful displays of cut fruit fanned out across porcelain platters. Were anyone to pass by and look in through the tall, arched windows, they might wonder at the unusual range of diversity represented there. But there'd be no reason to consider anything more taking place than friends coming together to share a meal. In fact, that was the case, although the friendships had been forged through much greater spans of time and origins more exotic than anyone could possibly imagine.

Paul's guests were seated and comfortable, their plates holding hors d'oeuvres and their glasses of wine full. They'd relaxed and chatted for the last half-hour, but now it was time to discuss the reason they'd gathered. Paul looked around the table and waited. Soon, conversations slowly dropped off and all eyes turned to him.

There were five others present. Claudia, Harrison, Oliver, Valerie and Trevor. Paul had known them by these names for a long time, but he'd known them to have others in the past. Just as he'd known them to appear differently.

For now, he saw two women, one white and one Asian. He saw three men, one black, one Middle-Eastern and one of mixed race. Ironically, their kind was unique on the planet in that, to them, race didn't matter. Nor gender. They considered these things fluid, inconsequential, instead recognizing what lay within. What humans might call spirit, although Paul well knew that, in their case, that word wouldn't be used to describe them. "Parasite" might be the term more likely applied.

"As you know, she's coming into her powers," Paul said. "A little at a time, but it's becoming clear."

"I felt it," Trevor said. "Last night."

"There's no doubt, she's getting stronger," Valerie said.

The others nodded, indicating that they too had felt the most recent resonances. In fact, it was the occurrence two nights ago which had drawn Paul in Autumn's direction once more. It had been entirely a hunch, but he'd felt certain another would soon follow. He hadn't been wrong.

"Which means that we need to make a decision," Paul said. The unstated implication, of course, was that he'd already made one and now it was time to see if they agreed.

"How much does she know?" The question came from Oliver, and Paul saw in his eyes that he already knew the answer.

Paul gestured dismissively. "As you suspect, so far she only has the most vague sense of what she can do."

Claudia leaned in to face the group. "But, obviously, recent circumstances have created considerably more concern than we've had to face in a while."

Glances were exchanged at her comment. They all understood what she meant. The concern was ongoing, although lately pressure had been building.

"The fact is, she may never know what she's capable of," Paul said. "In the past, it would almost be guaranteed."

The others nodded concurrence.

"Exactly," Trevor said. "How long has it been since one of them truly knew?"

Claudia took the moment to remind the others that, in his decision, Paul wasn't alone. "A very long time," she said. "It's part of what we've had to consider."

Despite their relationship, Claudia hadn't hesitated to disagree with Paul in the past. Not when her viewpoint differed. As a result, her alliance with him on this matter would be taken that much more seriously.

"I can't recall the last time one of them was a serious threat," Valerie said.

"All the more reason why she could be now," Paul said. "In a sense, the timing couldn't be more fortunate. Just think how long it could be until we have another opportunity. Fifty years? One hundred? I think we should act while we still can."

The possibility had been discussed before, but only as a matter of speculation. Now, objections were voiced around the table. Harrison set down his wine glass so hard that the stem snapped off. He held the bowl as wine dribbled across his fingers like blood from a wound.

Paul held up a hand to regain their attention. "There's an aspect we haven't yet discussed. Mostly, because we needed to be sure, but it appears that someone is helping her."

"Who?" Valerie asked, her frown deepening. "Helping her how?"

"A man named Ian," Claudia said. "A private investigator. From what we've gathered, he seems to have made a connection."

Before voices could rise again, Paul explained. "As we suspected, it was only a matter of time before the other faction got noticed."

"Especially if, as we believe may be the case," Claudia said, gesturing to the plates of food displayed before them, "it's been served up on a platter."

"Which is exactly why we've reached this point of impasse," Trevor said.

Valerie shifted her attention to Trevor. "True, but all that aside, our hosts long ago decided we don't exist."

"Unfortunately, we can't rely on that any longer," Claudia said.

"Thanks to the others," Oliver said.

"Exactly," Harrison muttered, still clutching the bowl of his wineglass.

Paul decided not to pursue the point. Not because it wasn't true, but simply because it had been discussed so many times in the past. "There are two key factors at work," he said, "making this a uniquely challenging situation. Or, opportunity, depending on your point of view. The first is that this man, Ian, feels convinced that he's noticed a pattern. Under normal circumstances,

Autumn would likely dismiss his claims. Or, quite possibly, consider them both equally deluded. Except for the fact that her own sister vanished when she was a child."

Paul looked around the table again to make his meaning clear.

"A child," Trevor said.

Paul nodded. "She was eleven at the time."

Valerie narrowed her eyes as she peered into Paul's. "Are you saying what I think you're saying?"

"I'm afraid so," Paul said. "I suspect the others detected the resonances long before we did. Fifteen years before, to be exact."

Harrison shook his head. "It's not possible. Has it ever even happened?"

Trevor picked up Harrison's point. "The odds against that have to be astronomical. Are you suggesting both sisters might be realm watchers?"

Paul glanced around the table again. "That's what I believe. Which is why I think we have no choice but to act preemptively."

"I take it you mean occupy her," Valerie said. She glanced down at the table before adding, "Or kill her, if need be."

"That might have been an option," Paul said. "But by all accounts she should have already died." Glances volleyed back and forth across the table, telling Paul that his guests understood his meaning. "Instead, I'm suggesting that we tell Ms. Winters exactly what she is before she discovers it for herself."

CHAPTER 14

I walk toward the front door bearing gifts, one each for Zelda and Ethan, as well as a long-overdue housewarming gift. Zach and Ellen smile through the front door window and I see the tops of Zelda's and Ethan's heads bobbing up and down as they try to get a peek. Their excited clamoring comes to me muffled through the door.

The door swings open and I step inside, the guilt and hesitation melting away as little arms wrap around my legs and bigger arms pull me into a hug, first Zach and then Ellen.

"Are those presents for us?" Zelda stares up at me, her giant green eyes framed by curly red hair.

Ethan stands a head shorter than his sister, looking like a Zach mini-me with his trusting face and stocky build.

"Manners, guys," Ellen says.

"Geez, at least let her get into the house," Zach says.

He swings the door closed and I crouch down in front of my niece and nephew. I hold out the bag of gifts and say, "What makes you think one of these is for you?"

Ethan stands on his tip-toes, trying to look into the bag while Zelda points knowingly. "I see Snoopy paper!" she says.

"Snoopy!" Ethan says, giving me the impression he'd be happy enough with just the gift wrap.

I nod, pretending to give that some thought, then look at them seriously. "Hmm, that is pretty observant of you. But how do you know those aren't for your parents?"

"I see another one with blue paper!" Zelda says.

"Blue paper!" Ethan says.

I glance up at Zach and Ellen. "Kind of getting the feeling these two work as a team."

"For now," Ellen says.

"Yeah, give them a few years," Zach says. Maybe he's remembering sibling rivalry, or maybe just predicting the future. Either way, his eyes show nothing short of happiness in this moment and I'm already glad I came.

We watch as Zelda and Ethan tear open their gifts of floppy-eared stuffed puppies, their faces lighting up. They charge at me with more hugs, nearly knocking me over before scampering off toward the family room, Ethan's dog barking and chasing after Zelda's as they hold them out.

I straighten up to take the place in, glancing into the living room where I see new furniture and framed photos lining the mantel. "This is really nice," I say.

"Thanks, we love it," Ellen says.

"Also got a good deal on it," Zach says, always humble. He told me before that the old townhouse had been selling as-is, put on the market as a fixer-upper by a couple who'd lived there for only a year before deciding to move on. A sweet deal for someone with the right skills, or a potential money pit for someone unrealistic about the amount of work to be done. For Zach and Ellen, the place had been a perfect opportunity since, clearly, he more than knew his way around construction and she was pretty handy herself. On top of which, they'd been dreaming of buying a townhouse in the Museum District but had assumed it to be way out of reach. Now, here they were creating their dream home and their future.

I do a quick check of their eyes, but if that thing Zach mentioned in one of our previous phone calls has been causing any serious problems it doesn't show in their expressions.

"Come on, check out the kitchen," Zach says.

I follow them down the hall, past the dining room and into their gleaming new kitchen. Like all of the townhouses I've been in, the kitchen isn't huge but theirs is bright and sunny, with windows looking out onto a screened back porch. Pendant lights hang above shiny granite counters that I'm guessing they just installed, and cobalt glassware sits framed within glass-fronted custom cabinetry. Crayon drawings of personified, smiling suns and flowers adorn their refrigerator.

"Guys, this is beautiful," I say.

Zach and Ellen beam back at me, rightfully proud homeowners.

"Thanks," Zach says. "Banged the crap out of my hand installing that stupid dishwasher." He holds up a thick-fingered paw to show me bruises.

"Well, honey," Ellen says. "I'm pretty sure it says in the installation instructions not to shove it with your hip and trap your hand in next to it."

"Hey, I thought it would clear."

"Yes, you have such dainty hands, dear." Ellen rolls her eyes good-naturedly and turns to me. "It's really good to see you."

"You too," I say. "Oh, here. I got you something."

I pull the remaining gift from the bag and they unwrap the vase I chose at Pottery Barn. It's cobalt blue to go with their glassware.

Ellen cradles the vase in her hands. "It's beautiful! We have just the spot for it."

"It's really nice," Zach says. "Thank you."

Ellen opens one of the cabinets and rearranges a few items. A moment later, my gift has claimed prime real estate in their display, looking like it was always meant to be there. Ellen comes over and gives me another hug. "Thank you," she whispers into my ear. She draws away again and says, "You still sure about this? They can keep you pretty darned busy."

"Definitely," I say.

"Okay, I just have to run upstairs for a sec and then we can go."

Ellen leaves the room and it's just me and Zach. "Can I get you anything?" he says. "Something to drink, maybe?"

Zach's not the indirect type, but part of me still wonders if it might be a test. Not that I blame him. They're trusting me to look after their kids, and it wouldn't surprise me if my mother might have mentioned my drinking at some point.

"Got any Diet Pepsi?" I say.

Zach looks momentarily confused. For him, that's lady territory. I'm not sure, but I think he also looks relieved. He checks the fridge and says, "Yeah, we do.

He goes to get me a glass but I say, "Can's fine. Don't worry about it."

Zach shrugs and passes me the can of soda. "You sure?"

I pop the can and take a sip. "Totally. So, any more of that stuff going on around here?"

It's just something he told me about not long after they moved into the house. A total coincidence, since he has no way of knowing that I see ghosts. I never told him, but it's another reason why I wanted to come here tonight. Mostly, I wanted to see Zelda and Ethan—I wasn't lying to myself about that—but it also occurred to me that I might have the chance to be sure about things while also helping out Zach and his family.

Zach hesitates, as if he's a little embarrassed now that we're face to face. "Yeah, a little. I don't know, maybe it's our imagination."

"It's pretty weird," I say, trying to keep it casual. "That thing you told me about stuff moving around."

Zach lowers his voice for the kids' sake, although they've already got the TV cranked in the other room. "We keep finding drawers left open and stuff sitting out on the counters. Knives a couple of times. It's kind of concerning." He gestures to the cabinets they just installed. "And we put safety locks on all of them. I don't know what to think."

I know better, but I still ask. "You don't think it might have been one of you guys?"

He shakes his head. "I don't know. The first couple of times, sure. I figured Ellen just forgot and she thought it was me. Yeah, it's pretty strange."

"It's probably nothing," I say, which makes no sense. But I can see that it bothers him. After all, they just sank their savings into getting this place.

Zach glances out the window. "Zelda said something about seeing some lady. She asked if it was my grandmother."

My heartbeat kicks up a notch at the thought. "Was she scared?"

"Didn't seem to be. I don't know…maybe she just had a dream or something."

"What are you guys talking about?" Ellen comes back into the kitchen as she finishes putting on her earrings.

Zach's eyes dart away from mine and I get it. He doesn't want things ruined for Ellen. I'm sure he's more than a little relieved at changing the subject too.

"I was just telling Autumn not to let those two talk her into staying up past eight," he says. "Eight-thirty at the latest."

Ellen laughs. "No kidding. Those two know how to work a room." She checks her purse and turns to me again. "Thank you so much. We haven't been out in forever."

"We'll just grab some dinner, see the movie, and come straight home," Zach says.

"Take your time and have fun," I say.

"Call if you need us," Ellen says.

"We'll be fine." I keep my eyes on theirs, forcing myself not to look at the woman who just crossed through the wall. She stands by the cellar door watching us, thinking no one can see her.

~~~

It's a good thing that I've never seen *Frozen* before since Zelda and Ethan are only half way through it when I join them in the family room and, after an ice cream break, they want to watch it again.

"So you can see the beginning," Zelda says, the wily little thing.

It's not like I don't see the wheels spinning behind those green eyes but I'm more than happy to go along with the plan. For one thing, she's got the world's cutest smile and Ethan is already jumping on the sofa with excitement at the idea. Which also tells me that this is where Zach and Ellen would have countered with an alternate plan such as baths and reading. But, hey, I'm their only aunt and I've missed way too many chances to spoil them.

I check my watch. Almost seven so, okay, bed by nine at the latest. "Pajamas first," I say, so they don't think they can walk all over me.

"How about after the movie?" Zelda says. "We'll be fast!"

"Okay," I say, and I can see where this is going in the years ahead.

The second viewing is well worth it, though. By the time Demi Levato belts out "Let it Go" again, the three of us are nestled on the couch together, Ethan snoozing with his head in my lap and Zelda gazing dreamy-eyed with her mouth hanging open.

As it turns out, Zelda outmaneuvered me even better than I thought. They both claim to be so tired that the only way I can get them both to brush their teeth and change into pajamas is by bribing them with the promise of reading them both a story. Which I do, *Goodnight Moon* being a bit of letdown after the animated spectacle of *Frozen*. Finally, I carry Ethan to his bedroom and tuck him in, then return to Zelda's room to kiss her and turn off the light.

She wraps me in a hug, the skin of her arms like warm silk against my neck. "I'm glad you came back," she whispers.

My eyes go moist and I'm not sure what to say. Somehow, I was hoping she didn't know but, of course, she must. I'm not sure how Zach and Ellen handled it but she's five—it's not like she could have remained totally oblivious to the fact that her father lost his brother and me my husband.

"I'm sorry," I say, smoothing her hair back from her forehead. "I won't go away again."

"I know," she says. "You're different now. I can feel it."

She yawns, closes her eyes and rolls onto her side. She's asleep before I get to my feet, already drifting away to a place where only children get to visit in their dreams.

The woman is still in the kitchen when I get there, which I pretty much expected. She stands in the same spot where she stood watching when Zach and Ellen were leaving, and where I saw her again later while the kids had their ice cream. I pick up the bowls from the table, take them to the counter and wait while filling the sink with water. I face the window, seeing my own reflection. I don't see her there, but I feel her as she hovers closer. I wait until she's right next to me, then turn to her.

"It's a nice kitchen," I say. "Do you like it?"

Her eyes widen and she steps back, flickering and then appearing again a couple of feet away. She says nothing.

I squirt some dishwashing liquid into the sink and submerge the bowls. I wait until she draws closer again. "Why are you still here?"

She stares at me, stunned. She parts her lips to speak but no words come.

"How long has it been?" I say.

She shakes her head.

"Did something happen here? To you? Why don't you leave?"

She flickers back, then forward again, and I wonder how long it's been since she's had any sort of contact. She barely manifests. I keep waiting and she points at the sink.

Her chin trembles, her mouth opens and finally she speaks. "Mine," she says.

I shake my head. "The sink is yours? I don't understand."

But I do. I understand.

She wheels about and points at the stove. "Mine."

"But that's not yours," I say. "That's new. Yours is gone, right?"

She looks at me and, after a moment, nods.

This is an old Richmond townhouse, built in the early 1900s. It's impossible to say what stood here before, but there's no doubt that people have lived, and died, in this location for a very long time.

"This was your kitchen, wasn't it?" I say.

She keeps her eyes on mine. Finally, she manages to get out more than one word. "People keep coming in."

I want to ask if she has any idea how long it's been, if she knows that she's dead. Clearly, she's remained here for some reason. "Why do you keep waiting?" I say.

"Richard," she says. "I made his dinners here."

The memories flood into me, her memories. I see her wearing a floral cotton dress and a light green apron. She's young and freckled and pretty, her auburn hair pulled back from a glowing face. I see him too—tall with his hair cropped short, wearing a crisp uniform. He pulls her into a hug and whispers a promise.

I'll come back.

But he never did.

I step toward her. "Oh, sweetie. How old are you?"

She looks at me through ancient eyes, her face an alabaster mask of folds and wrinkles. "Nineteen," she says. "We were going to have children."

I can't help it. I start to cry, tears running down my face. "Do you want to go to him?"

She stares at me, thinking it's not possible.

"What's your name?"

"Sherry," she says. "I'm Sherry."

Before I speak again, I wait to be sure. I need to know that I didn't dream it before. That I'm not crazy. But that's why I came here. To be around people I know, living people with beating hearts and a future. I needed to ground this thing, whatever it is, in a place where I thought I might be able to safely, clearly, see both sides of it. I do now and I feel the pulsing buzz of energy starting to build within me.

Zelda was right. I'm different now.

I ask the question again. "Do you want to go to him?"

Tears run down her face now too as she reaches out to me. "Yes, please. I want to see my parents again too. And my sisters."

I reach out and open my hands. We both watch as the light spreads toward her.

CHAPTER 15

The next afternoon, Ian drives us across town and it feels strange to be sitting in the passenger seat beside him. It's only in that moment that I realize that, since Justin died, I haven't once been in a car unless I'm driving. Maybe it's fear, trauma or a control thing. I don't know. It also occurs to me that I haven't been in a space this small, this intimate, with a man since then either. I keep looking out the window like I've never seen Richmond before, pretending I can't smell the scent of him—a mix of pine, mint and something that reminds me of grass after rain—which I guess must be the combination of his soap, shampoo and deodorant. The problem is, I don't want to like the smell of him but I do. Just as I like the way he glides the car along, his hand spread at the wheel and his eyes watchfully scanning, as he both relaxes and concentrates at the same time.

"You didn't tell me before," I say, to break the silence that he doesn't seem to notice, "how long were you a cop?"

"About six years, start to finish."

Shit, really? Six years ago I was a junior in college.

Ian glances over and lifts an eyebrow, as if he heard my thought. Right, psychic, I think. Almost forgot that part.

"I'm thirty-four," he says. "You?"

"Twenty-seven."

He nods and keeps driving.

"You knew that, didn't you?"

"Yeah, I did."

"So, why did you ask?"

He checks his rearview mirror and changes lanes. "Just being sure. You look really young. You know that, right?"

I've heard this before, many times. Some people seem mystified, others envious, but I look way younger than I actually am, like I stopped aging when I reached eighteen.

"I *feel* old," I say.

Ian chuckles. "I hear you."

I glance out the window, thinking about cracking it open. Not because I'm hot but just because I feel fidgety. "You mentioned becoming obsessed with those cases. But did you also leave the force because of the thing?"

That smile plays at the corner of his mouth again. "The thing?"

"You know what I mean."

"I do," he says, "but for some reason, I imagined a monster rising out of a swamp."

"I bet it feels that way sometimes."

He laughs. "True enough. But that monster saved my life a few times."

"In Iraq," I say.

"And a few other times," Ian says. "Maybe just not quite as literally. It just took me a while to figure it out. To listen."

"Why?"

"You know," he says.

"Because it's scary."

He reaches out without even appearing to think about it. He offers his closed fist and I bump it.

"Boom," I say.

"Yep, boom," he says. "Talk to all the mountain climbers, sailors and astronauts. Where would we be without scary?"

I think about that for a moment. "Is that what we are, explorers?"

Ian pulls the car into the police station parking lot and kills the engine. "Me? Yes. Just finding my way. As for you, I get the feeling you've been there before. I'm just here to remind you how to get back again."

~~~

Ian tells a uniformed young woman why we're there and she calls back to double-check. We thank her and walk down a hall lined with framed photos of more uniformed men and women, both white and black, all of them honored in this hall for either dying in service or being decorated. Soon, we come to an office and the man behind the desk waves us in. He looks to be pushing fifty, thin and going bald. He's on the phone but gestures to two chairs, signaling us to sit. He continues to listen and jot down notes for another minute before ending his call and turning his attention to Ian.

"Yeah, it's interesting," he says, his forefinger tapping a manila folder on the desk. "How did you know?"

Ian shrugs. "Just a feeling."

The man nods. "Of course. How's that working out for you these days?"

"Debatable."

The man laughs and turns his gaze to me. "Steve Flynn," he says, reaching across the desk to shake my hand.

"Autumn Winters," I say.

He keeps his eyes on mine and lifts an eyebrow.

"Married name," I say.

He nods. "Ah, gotcha. Ian says you're working the case with him."

It's a strange thing to hear, made even more strange because it's essentially true. I have no idea how much Ian might have told him, but I'm guessing not all that much. Who'd believe it? Thankfully, Ian gets me off the hook.

"Autumn's the one who told me to check for the tattoos," he says.

Needless to say, Ian doesn't mention that I got the idea from talking to a disembodied spirit of a missing girl.

Steve keeps his eyes on mine. "Just a feeling?"

I shrug. "Something like that."

"Okay, sure. I won't ask any more. But it was a good hunch."

He flips open the folder and spins it around. I wasn't quite ready for what I see, but I guess I should have been. Ian's old partner is a detective, after all. It's not like he spends his days handing out parking tickets. The photo shows the face of a woman, probably somewhere near thirty-five but it's hard to be sure. It's not exactly a flattering photo since she's both very pale and very dead.

"This is the one they found out by the Diamond," Steve says. "Overdose, for sure. Heroin. A lot." He shakes his head, confused. "As in, no one would even think about it unless dying was the entire point. Just no way it was an accident. Basically, if this was a gunshot suicide, it would be like blowing your head off three times. I double-checked with the ME and she confirmed. Her heart should have stopped on round one."

"This is the woman from Ohio," Ian says.

"Right, exactly," Steve says. "Janet Crowley. Some relatives saw her picture on the internet after we posted it."

Ian glances at me and I know what he's thinking. Janet Crowley went missing sometime in the past without a trace. Twenty years later she turns up here. Dead.

"You two done not talking?" Steve says.

Ian grins. "Sorry."

Steve shakes his head. "Psychics. Like it's not weird enough out there." He slides the top photo aside to reveal another, this time showing a close-up of a tattoo on milky flesh.

I perch forward and squint, not quite sure what I'm seeing. Ian does the same.

"Inner thigh." Steve shrugs. "Presumably meant for special friends."

Ian stares intently and I'm guessing it has nothing to do with where the tattoo shows on the body. I don't know him well, but I know him better than that just on instinct. I turn my attention back to the tattoo and find myself staring as well. I see what look like symbols of some sort, or letters. I'm just not sure. The lines are carefully drawn, the curves precisely rendered and incredibly ornate. The impression I get is that I'm seeing an exotic language that I can't read.

Steve places his index finger on top of the photo as if to slide it aside. He makes eye contact with me. "Have you seen many post-mortem images, Ms. Winters?"

I think about splitting hairs and asking if seeing ghosts counts. "Typically, I try to avoid it," I say.

"You might want to brace yourself." He reveals another photo, this one showing a pale face disfigured by bloating. My stomach lurches and I have to look away.

I remember what Ian told me, that she'd been found floating in the river. "Emily Richards," I say.

"None other," Steve says. "Hard to believe, but at the time of her disappearance she was reported to have been exceptionally attractive. Another overdose victim, as it happens."

I shake my head, confused. "I thought she drowned."

"First, she overdosed. Or, more than likely, someone overdosed her. I can't speak for Janet Crowley there but, by all accounts Emily Richards had no issues with substances of any kind. Her family and friends said she was a light drinker, at most. Needless to say, foul play was suspected but, so far, no leads. By the way, no sign of sexual assault either so the most likely motive was also ruled out." This time, Steve flips the photo over. Out of kindness, presumably. He slides another photo toward us and turns his attention to Ian. "And there's your tattoo again. On the underside of her forearm this time but, still. What are the odds?"

Ian and I both lean forward to look since whoever took the photo didn't shoot nearly as close. Even from a distance, though, it's plain to see that the tattoo is an exact match.

"Exactly, what are the odds?" Ian says. "Have you ever seen that kind of tattoo before?

Steve shakes his head. "No, but there are a lot of tattoos in the world."

"But still."

Steve straightens the photos and slides them back into the folder. "True. It's not like we're talking about shamrocks or dragonflies. That particular design does seem a little obscure."

Ian nods toward the folder. "Can I keep those?"

"What are friends for?" Steve slides the folder across the desk. "By the way, who's the client? You already worked the Richards case."

Ian nods but doesn't say anything, regret written in his expression. I wonder if he blames himself for what happened or if it's just a matter of having come close. "No client," he says, getting to his feet. "Like I said before, I just got a feeling about something."

Steve chuckles and shakes his head. "Probably better off not knowing."

~~~

"What you said in there isn't really true," I say, as Ian starts the car to take me home.

Ian puts the car in drive but looks over at me. "How's that?"

"Well, you do sort of have a client."

"Rachel Joyner, you mean. I agree but, as you can imagine, I was slightly hesitant to open that can of worms. At this point, RPD is all over that case and I don't imagine my looking into it would sit well."

"And it's not like you can exactly tell them that you know someone who's seen her."

"Exactly. There's that world" –Ian gestures toward the window—"and then there's the one we walk around in. You way more than me—and something tells me you haven't shared the half of it yet—but, either way, it doesn't exist to most of the guys I used to know. Steve's a good guy. Open minded, as much as possible. But that doesn't mean he didn't consider reporting me as being a liability when I let on that I sometimes know things I shouldn't be able to know. I'm pretty sure at first he thought I might be losing my shit."

I think back to the rapport between Ian and Steve, nothing in that dynamic suggesting Steve didn't both respect Ian and take him seriously. He wasn't entirely comfortable with the idea of psychic abilities, I could tell, but he didn't dismiss the idea either. It's my turn to have a feeling about something. "What happened? You changed his mind somehow, didn't you?"

"Not that I'd planned to but that was the result," Ian says. "Steve started to guess something was going on with me. I just had a way of looking in places other people hadn't thought to look and finding things no one knew we were looking for. You do that enough times and your partner is going to notice. Proximity is bound to do that but it works both ways, of course."

He says it like I know and, the thing is, it does make sense. While in the past I might have been on the fence, at best, now I have no doubt. "You saw something about him."

Ian glances out at the parking lot, past the squad cars and unmarked vehicles. "He was worried about his daughter. She was fifteen at the time, the light of his life. He never told me anything was wrong but somehow I knew. One day, I got a flash on her. A series of images and feelings all pointing to the same thing. I couldn't ignore it so I told Steve he needed to check in her dresser, bottom drawer. What do you think he found?"

I look over at him. "No idea."

"I don't believe you," Ian says. "No way someone who has what you've got going on can't tap into this. You can see it, can't you?"

As soon as he says it, I realize it's true. But I just figured it for being my imagination. "A phone?"

"Exactly. A burner phone she got from some creep who turned her onto drugs and way more. The guy was nineteen."

"Something tells me that didn't end well. For the record, that's just basic assumption."

"You assumed right," Ian says, "although Steve didn't share the details. He just thanked me and, after that, well, things were okay between us again for the time I remained on the force. Like I said, he's a good guy."

"I can tell. So, what's the next step?"

"Well, I was planning on driving you home."

"Rethink that plan," I say. "For now, I'm your new partner. By the way, did you see that coming?"

Ian looks over at me and grins. "Have to admit, I didn't."

CHAPTER 16

It turns out that neither one of us had lunch so we drive down Broad looking for a place to eat. As we cruise along, it occurs to me that this will also be the first time in over a year that I've gone out to lunch with someone other than Molly. Not to mention someone who's a guy and not Justin. I try not to overthink it since, obviously, if we're going to be partners then we'll be spending time together.

"Are you a vegetarian?" Ian asks.

"Been thinking about it," I say, which is only half-true. I *have* thought about it, which isn't exactly the same thing. "What about you?"

Ian chuckles. "I've been thinking about it too."

I see where he's going with this, but I still take the bait. "For how long?"

"I don't know, five years maybe?"

I find myself chuckling too. "Yeah, me too. That's a lot of bacon under the bridge."

"Exactly. So, I'm thinking we eat there while we continue to ponder healthier future eating."

I follow Ian's gaze to where, across the street, I see a place called Boulevard Burger and Brew. "Ever been there before?"

Ian stops at the light and signals to turn. "Probably more than I should admit. It's a little too conveniently located, considering my office is about a mile away. They also have amazing burgers."

"A place designed for crushing all hopes of future vegetarianism," I say.

"Definitely a great place to make you stop thinking about it, at least."

We park, go inside and find we're lucky to even get a table. It's four o'clock on a weekday and the place is packed. I check out the menu and consider my burger options. I also can't help but notice that the menu logo features a Vargas style illustration of a woman with a lot of tattoos. The place is manned mostly by young, hipster types so it doesn't surprise me to see that our waitress bears a number of tattoos on her arms as well. Evidently, it's part of the theme.

"Lots of ink going on here," I observe.

"Purely coincidental," Ian says. "But maybe we should run a few cadaver photos past the wait staff?"

Maybe it's just the stress and weirdness of the last couple of days but I have to laugh. "Probably not the best idea if you intend to remain a regular."

"True," Ian says. "Might go over as being a bit morbid. Maybe we should take it someplace else."

"Like where?"

Ian lifts his eyebrows, a glint of amusement in his eyes, then rolls up his sleeve to reveal a tattoo of an owl curled around itself to create a yin-yang pattern. "Just for the sake of thematic cohesiveness," he says. "I was thinking of maybe starting where I got this."

"Nice," I say, admiring the artwork. "So, you know a guy."

"Who might know a guy," Ian says.

"I'm new at this, after all, but do the odds seem a little unlikely?"

Ian nods. "Extremely. But one thing I've learned by now is to start with what you have. From there, sometimes it keeps going. Not always. What about you? If I'm not mistaken, you were an art student not long ago. Isn't it basically required?"

My face grows a little warm as I involuntarily blush. I tap my ribcage, not quite as close to the underside of my breast as where I actually have the tattoo. "Dragonfly," I admit.

Ian hesitates, then bursts out laughing. He raises his eyebrows again. "Do you mind if I share that one with Steve later?"

"Yes!" I feel my face redden a little more. "I was nineteen at the time. It's not like I knew that dragonflies were cliché. Anyway, whatever, I like my dragonfly."

"I'm sure it's a very nice dragonfly," Ian says, as the waitress drops our food off.

I check to be sure, but I sense no subtext in his reassurance. I can tell he's just being nice. The fact is, I get the impression that, most of the time, Ian lives in the past. Something tells me it's been a long time since he was interested in anyone other than the girl who got suddenly taken from his life.

"Here, try these." Ian slides a basket my way.

He ordered the fried mac and cheese appetizer and I had no idea what that might be about. I take a bite out of deep-fried breaded pasta triangle topped with ranch dressing and full of a melted mix of gooey cheese.

"Oh, my God," I say. "This is incredible!"

"Totally vegetarian, by the way," Ian says. "Just realized that. So, you know a guy too."

It takes me a moment before I catch his meaning. "Oh, right. It was a long time ago. Some place called Inked In, on Cary Street."

I swallow what's left of his first fried mac and cheese. "Well, I guess it must be our day for coincidences."

"How do you figure?"

"We both know the same guy."

~~~

I can't exactly say that Inked In is just like I remember it since I both got my tattoo a long time ago and, yes, there was also a certain amount of liquid courage involved. Back then, I wasn't really much of a drinker. Actually, compared to most of the kids who lived in my dorm, I was pretty much a lightweight. But the thought of that little needle stabbing me over and over, along with the fact that I'd be living with my decision for the rest of my life, had required a little numbing up front.

Still, it's the same little shop in the same location on Cary Street. When Ian and I come through the front door, the owner looks up from behind the counter, where he sits looking at his phone. Him, I do remember, for being both gentle and kind and for his completely bald head, bright red beard and black-framed glasses. He just has one of those faces I'd always be able to pick out of a crowd. I haven't thought of him in years but his name comes back to me now too. Phillip Aznavorian.

"How are you two do—" Phillip's eyes flick back and forth between me and Ian. "Hey, wait."

Ian approaches the counter and offers his hand. "Hey, Phil, how's it going?"

A smile lights up his face. "Sean, right?"

"Ian."

"Right, Ian. Sure." His eyes travel back and forth between us again. "Wait, were you two... Autumn, right?"

I nudge Ian with my elbow. "Guess I'm just more memorable."

"But if I'm not mistaken, I saw you"—Phillip turns his attention to Ian—"like fifteen years ago and you"—he turns his attention to me—"something like ten. Am I getting that about right?"

"Twelve," Ian says.

"Eight," I say.

In its awkwardness, it's a funny moment and we all start laughing.

"Okay, whatever." Phillip's face reddens, even the dome of his skull blushing a little. "Close enough. Good to see you guys. Did you two meet and decide it was time for some new body art or what's the deal?"

Ian shrugs. "More like we're curious about something. We wanted to see what you thought."

"Okay…" Phillip draws the word out, understandably confused. He glances at the notebook in Ian's hand, maybe noticing it for the first time or just making the logical connection that it must factor in somehow.

This is something Ian and I talked about before leaving the restaurant, that we better play our cards pretty close to the vest. Otherwise, and quite understandably, anyone we ask would be reluctant for fear of being somehow implicated.

"It's about this tattoo," Ian says. He sets the notebook on the counter and flips it open to where I drew a copy of the design. Six years of art school paid off, at least in this instant.

Phillip perches forward to study the sweeping arcs and ornate loops of the symbols. "What is that, like Sanskrit or something?"

Ian shrugs. "No idea. Is that what it looks like to you?"

Philip pulls a pair of reading glasses out from behind the counter and slips them on for a closer look. "You know what it reminds me of? An alien alphabet."

I shake my head, making sure I heard right. "Alien alphabet?"

Phillip laughs. "Yeah, it's a gamer thing. You can add alien alphabets to some games to make them more authentic. I don't know. Something about this design reminds me of those. Anyway, what's the deal?"

"You or me?" Ian says.

"Oh, God. You," I say.

"Well, Autumn met this girl at a party. They had a few drinks and one thing led to another…"

"Shit, this is so embarrassing," I say, covering my face in my hands.

"Then, as it turns out, the girl had to leave suddenly when a significant someone else turned up."

"Oh, got it!" Philip said. "You never got her info!"

I wince. "Yeah. But she had that cool tattoo. I was thinking maybe if I…"

Phillip's eyes go back and forth between us again. "I just figured you two were…"

Ian shakes his head. "No, we just work together."

"Got it. Cool." Phillip looks at me again. "Kind of like that old movie. What was it called? Desperately Seeking Susan or something. Does that sound right?"

I have no idea if he means the movie title or my emotional situation but it's not like it matters. "Yeah, I think so."

Phillip glances at the drawing again. "Dude, the odds are like a million to one. Couldn't you just ask someone at the party?"

"It's complicated," I say.

Phillip thinks about that for a moment, then nods. "Gotcha. I mean, I could ask around, I guess. It is a pretty unique design."

And not one you want to see all that often, evidently. "That would be awesome," I say.

"Should I call you if something comes up?"

"Maybe call me." Ian tears out the drawing and writes down his phone number at the top. "I'm sort of acting as wingman on this."

Phillip glances at me again.

"Like I said, it's complicated," I say.

~~~

By the time Ian drives me back home, it's already dark. I look up at the moon rising into the sky, thinking how strange it is that, just a month or so ago, the sun would have been another hour from setting.

"That was interesting, what Phil said about the Sanskrit thing. It made me think of something else we might try." Ian stops at a red light. "I have a friend who studied Theology. She might know what those symbols mean."

"Worth a try, definitely," I say. "What's she doing now?"

"My friend? According to Facebook, she's in corporate communications, whatever that means."

"See, that's why I stuck with an Art degree."

Ian hesitates, then looks over to see if I'm serious. I raise my eyebrows and he laughs. You have to hand it to him for being diplomatic. "Well, you didn't finish yet, right?"

Which he knows, of course. It bothered me before, the idea of him snooping around in my business. Not so much now that I both know him a little and understand why.

"Not yet," I say, once again leaving that door open, at least in my imagination.

"You will. You just needed some time."

My eyes go a little misty at the kindness of his tone. If anyone understands, I guess it must be him. Clearly, he needed time too, although why he spent it in Iraq makes me wonder. It seems like a dangerous thing to do just because he was confused. Then again, who am I to judge? Drinking yourself senseless for a year is plenty self-destructive too.

I turn to the window as I wipe my eyes. "Psychic prediction?"

"Call it a hunch. To judge by that drawing you did, I'd say you have some serious skill."

"Thanks."

"You were studying graphic design, right?"

"They call it Visual Communications. Same thing, basically." It's hard to believe that it's been just over a year since I was living that life, immersed in creativity every day. It seems like a century ago.

"Hey, you could open a tattoo studio," Ian says.

This time, I'm the one to check. Ian raises his eyebrows and I find myself laughing, just when I was about to be overcome with nostalgia. "Not sure I could handle those needles."

"Not to mention where you'd have to stick them," Ian says.

I laugh. "Right, that too. I'm on the next block."

"Okay, thanks."

"Wait, you didn't know?"

Ian shakes his head. "Well, I mean, I looked up your address but it's not like I came by or anything. It just seemed too, I don't know, intrusive."

Something in the way he says it tells me what he really means. It was over the line for him, coming to the place where I lived my life with Justin and where I'd since grieved alone.

He slows the car, looking for a place to park.

"This is fine," I say. "I can hop out here."

"You sure?"

Out of instinct, I scan the street. A couple walks past, heading in the opposite direction, their heads lowered as they talk. Two women about my age stand on the sidewalk, probably waiting for the bus. "Yeah, this is good."

The fact is, it's felt strange being with him all day and I just want to get out of the car. Not because I want to be alone. Instead, because I don't, which bothers me a little.

"I'll call that friend of mine," Ian says.

"Okay, sure. That sounds like a good plan." I know I told him we were partners in this, but now I'm not quite sure what that means. I get out of the car and swing the door closed without saying anything more. Kind of rude, I know, but right now I just don't care. Maybe I'll call him tomorrow. I don't look back and Ian drives off a moment later.

I'm almost at my door when the two women I saw before start walking in my direction. I look up to say hello, fishing for my keys, when they stop in front of me.

"Hey, Autumn. How's it going?" one of them says.

Her tone is friendly, casual, but I can't see their faces. The only light comes from a porch lamp and a streetlight behind them. One has long ringlets of curly hair, the other's hair is straight. They're both taller than me.

"Going good," I say. "Thanks."

I try to step around them but they block my path.

"What's the rush?" the other one says.

"Hey, fuck off." I grab the pepper spray from my bag, but it's snatched away before I even raise my hand. It happens so fast that I'm not even sure which one it was. It's like neither of them even moved. The canister clatters to the street a moment later, having spent more time in the air than in my grasp. My pulse escalates, my heartbeat thudding in my ears. "What do you want?"

I try to move but the same thing happens. I can't get past them and I step back. I should run, I know, but I stand frozen. Shock, I guess. Terror. I have no frame of reference and what does it matter? Where would I run to?

"I don't know, it seems like kind of a waste," the straight-haired one says. "She's sort of pretty."

"I know, she'd be good for Katherine," the other one says. "But whatever."

The straight-haired one turns to me and speaks softly. "We both think you're pretty. Do you think you're pretty?"

It's such an incongruous question, but for some reason I just stare at her. I find myself answering. "Not really."

She speaks again, using that same soothing tone. "Why? Because of that little scar on you cheek?"

I feel a pressure building behind my eyes. I imagine lights starting to pulse as the world around me blurs. "I got that in a car accident," I say.

The one with curly hair says, "You were in a car accident?"

Their voices numb me, like a narcotic humming through my brain. They stare and their eyes glow in the night, as if lit from within. One of them smiles and I imagine sharp, white teeth. This is a dream, I tell myself. It has to be a—

Suddenly, figures rush in as if from nowhere, silhouettes too fast to track. Bodies slam against bodies spinning the two women away. Steel glints, slashing quickly and something wet flecks against my face. I hear grunts and thrusts. One woman drops, then the other. The trance breaks and I cry out, my shriek piercing the night. A man steps over the bodies, walking toward me, not even winded. He's tall, his nearly white hair reflecting light, his face in shadow. Another stands back, a woman watching.

The man's eyes meet mine and they too glow pale gray. I think of a wolf. He speaks and it's like them, his voice soothing. "Ssh, it's okay," he says. "Everything's okay."

Lights start to pulse and flicker again. I want to look away, but I can't.

"It's better that you don't remember this," he says. "Not yet."

His head jerks away, then he turns to the other one. "No time," he says. "Now. Move."

They're gone so fast it's like they were never there. Within seconds, they blend in with the darkness. I can't

139

track them as lights grow bright against my eyes. I squint, standing frozen as the glare blinds me. Brakes squeal and I smell the burn of rubber. Sirens rise in the distance.

Someone grabs my arm and spins me. Only then do I realize that I still haven't moved, couldn't have. His voice is quiet but forceful. His eyes stare into mine and he pulls me forward.

"Get in the car," Ian says. "Get in, now!"

~~~

I expect Ian to tear out of there but he keeps himself under control, driving calmly and steadily. Behind us, the keen of sirens grows louder. Someone must have called the police, I think, probably when I screamed. It hits me then that a double-murder just took place in near total silence as well as a matter of seconds. The numbness wears off and I start trembling, then shaking uncontrollably. The tears come and, as I wipe them away, my fingers comes back slick and smeared. In the dark car, I stare down at my hand.

"Oh, my God. It's their blood." I should be screaming, but my words come out as little more than a whisper.

"I know," Ian says. "I saw that. Are you hurt? Are you bleeding?"

I shake my head. "No. They didn't..." It sinks in what they were probably going to do and I start shaking worse.

Ian turns on the heater. "You're in shock," he says. "Try to take deep breaths."

"Shouldn't we go back? The police."

Ian takes a left, still driving the speed limit, possibly a little below. "I know. I'm just hoping no one saw you out there. Either way, we can't risk them knowing you're alive."

"Who?"

He shakes his head. "That's just it, isn't it? But they knew where to find you."

I shudder, thinking about those two women blocking my path. "They knew my name."

"What did they say?"

I tell him what I remember, which isn't much. The comment about it being a waste, their flippant tone, the feeling that they didn't much care whether they were seen or heard. "What made you come back?"

Ian heaves a sigh and pats something between us on the console. "You forgot your notebook. Thank God. I was heading back when I heard someone scream. I wasn't sure what was going on and then I saw you standing there."

The other part comes back to me, about the two who showed up. I realize now that they were the couple I spotted before when I was getting out of Ian's car. "Just me? Did you see anyone else?"

"No. I mean at first I saw just you. Then I saw the bodies."

"Where are we going?"

"Away from here," he says. "If it's okay with you, I mean. I just don't think you should go back there right now."

Ian keeps driving, but he's waiting for me to answer.

"Yes," I say. "Keep going."

CHAPTER 17

Half an hour later, we pull into a driveway winding deep into the woods. Well, not so much a driveway as a rutted path. Ian's car jostles as we bump along through the dark. Two days ago, I was hesitant going with him to have a drink, and now here we are in the middle of nowhere.

"This is it," Ian says. "We'll be there in a sec."

"You live out here?"

"Well, I stay at my office sometimes. Like I told you, it's a little remote. Which is probably a good thing right now."

Ian told me about the place as we drove toward Powhatan, a cabin his grandparents left to his family. In the years since, his parents had moved to Maryland and his sister had gotten married, so Ian decided to live out here when he returned from Iraq. The privacy had appealed to him, he told me, along with the happy memories the place held. It had given him a new home and a place to heal.

When we get close enough to the cabin, sensor lights come on, illuminating the gravel driveway and path to the front door. A dog starts barking inside the house.

"That's Ollie," Ian says. "Don't worry, he's friendly."

"Shit, Louie!"

"Who's Louie?"

I'm almost surprised that he doesn't know. "My cat. He's—" I heave a sigh of relief. "It's okay, I filled his feeder this morning." *But if he dies again I won't be there to bring him back to life.* I don't share that thought with Ian. We have enough strangeness to sort through at the moment.

We go inside and Ian flicks the lights on as his Black Lab leaps and licks at both of us. "Down, boy," Ian says, turning to me to add, "He's a little excitable at first. He'll calm down in a sec."

Actually, getting to know Ollie is exactly what I need right now. The shock of what happened has only just worn off enough for me to stop trembling and petting a big, warm dog helps calm my nerves.

"He stays here alone?" I say.

"I come home most nights," Ian says, "but he has a door to get in and out."

I look around the cabin, which on the inside isn't as rustic as I imagined. Essentially, Ian has a nice and tidy little house out here in the woods, although his grandparents' presence still lingers. Lace curtains frame the windows and family photos line the mantel and seem to include a few generations.

I straighten up from kneeling next to Ollie. "I need to use your bathroom."

"Of course!" Ian says. "Sorry. I'll get you some towels."

"Towels?"

"Um…yeah, I was thinking you might want to…"

I shake my head, suddenly remembering that warm spray hitting my face. Ian managed to come up with a couple of napkins in the car, along with a bottle of water, which I used to clean up a little but, yes, a shower sounds like a very good idea.

Ian supplies me with towels and, as the water warms, I stare at a vivid reminder that what I experienced in front of my apartment building definitely wasn't a dream. I managed to get most of the blood off of my face, but my hair is matted in spots that I definitely don't want to touch. The front of my t-shirt is spattered, with what I wish was dark paint. Shit, clothes. What the hell am I going to do?

I peel off my shirt, drop my jeans to the floor and get out of my underwear. I'm standing naked at the mirror when Ian knocks on the door. My heart jumps and I instinctively cover myself.

"I'll leave some clothes out here in the hall," he says. "My sister keeps things here. My whole family does. Anyway, she's bigger than you but I think it might fit okay."

His footsteps fade and I get into the shower, letting the hot water flow over me. I tell myself I shouldn't look, but I still do as crimson spreads at my feet and swirls down the drain. Questions spin through my mind. Who were those women? What did they want? Actually, I'm pretty sure what they intended to do, but how did they find me and who sent them? Most importantly, who was it that stopped them? The glimpse I caught of the man's face comes back to me, his blonde hair and gray-blue eyes that reminded me of a wolf.

I wonder where I'd be right now if Ian hadn't come back and found me. Drunk in some bar, terrified to go home? Maybe, more than likely. I just don't know but I'm here now and, even though I'm afraid, I'm not nearly as terrified as I would be on my own. I stay in the shower until the water starts to cool, telling me I've probably been there a long time. I get out, wrap myself in a towel and crack open the door to retrieve the bundle from the hall. I find faded jeans and a long-sleeve t-shirt. Ian's right about the clothes being too big but they're clean and warm and I'm thankful to have them.

Ian's sitting at the kitchen table, a mug of tea in front of him and his laptop flipped open. His eyes meet mine as I come into the room. "What can I get for you?" he says. "I made some tea, but there's water, juice or coffee too. There's some wine here. Oh, my father keeps some whisky in the cabinet too for when they come down. He likes bourbon."

"Tea's fine," I say. "Actually, no. Fuck that. Bourbon."

Ian nods. "Yeah. No problem. Ice?"

"Do you have any beer?" I've never even had bourbon, but I was thinking the beer might chase it down.

He shakes his head.

"Sure, ice then. Thanks."

Ian gets up and makes the drink. He takes it to the table where I join him in front of the laptop, which is open to a news site. "I checked and it's just local right now," he says. "At this point, we know more than they do, but have a look if you want."

I sip the whisky and shudder as it burns down my throat. The warmth seeps into me almost immediately, though, and that part feels good. I read the news piece and Ian's right, there's not much other than the fact that they're reporting the mysterious killing of two women in my neighborhood. I check to be sure, reading through twice. No witnesses report having seen anything. The article says the police were called when someone heard a woman scream. The implication is that the scream probably came from one of the slain women.

"No identities, it says."

"Yeah, I know. Somehow, I'm not surprised," Ian says. "I didn't want to press before, but you seem a little better now. How were they killed? The article doesn't say."

The glint of steel flashing in the night plays before my eyes again. "Knife," I say. "Or maybe something bigger. A dagger, is that what it's called? Almost like a sword. It sounds crazy but I don't really know. It happened fast. Really fast."

The struggle too plays back, how quickly it happened. How efficiently those two women were cut down. It seems strange to me now that there had been no crying out, no pleading for mercy. Almost like there had been no fear.

"You okay?"

I take another sip of the bourbon and quiver less at the burn. " I think so. Not really. Shit."

"I know," Ian says. "But does it really surprise you?" My eyes widen and he says, "Not what you saw. This, all of it. Whatever this is, we're dealing with some serious shit. I know you know that."

"No kidding, but what the hell do we have to do with it?"

Ian's expression reflects what he was trying to tell me the other night. The part I just didn't want to hear. For him, it's a matter of coincidences being noticed, patterns observed. Those patterns led him to me. As far as I know, those patterns started with me and Cassie, bringing us to where we are now.

"I'm not sure," Ian says. "Does anyone know you've been with me?"

My pulse kicks up again. Here I sit after being attacked, alone with a man I don't know in the middle of the woods. What better question to ask than the one he just did?

"Oh, shit," Ian says. "I'm sorry. God. What I meant was that someone knew where to find you. I need to know whether we should keep moving."

I nod but the room is starting to swim. "Got it. No. I didn't tell anyone."

"Good," Ian says. "That's good. Hopefully, that means you're safe. I bet you're tired. Are you?"

I finish the bourbon. "You have no idea."

From there, it's basically a blank as Ian walks me toward a bedroom and I collapse onto a bed.

~~~

I wake up to the sound of a dog barking, having no idea where I am. It's pitch dark and I roll onto my back, my eyes flipping open. The dog barks again and I hear a voice. His voice. Then, I know.

"Ssh, Ollie. Quiet down."

I listen as Ollie does just the opposite, his barking getting more urgent. I go to the living room where Ian is still trying to calm down his dog. My heart starts pounding, the memories of what happened returning after being mercifully vanquished by sleep.

"What's going on?"

"I don't know. Something must be out there." He speaks calmly, but his eyes show apprehension.

"Does he usually act like this if something's out there?" Ollie has gone to the window, standing with his legs tensed as he keeps barking, now trying to see past closed mini-blinds.

"It's happened before. Could be a fox or maybe another dog."

My pulse starts to slow as I hope that's all it is.

"But we can't be sure about that." Ian remains still for a moment, then nods, having made a decision. He goes down the hall and comes back carrying guns, a rifle and a revolver. In the time that's passed, Ollie has kept jumping at the window, tearing at the mini-blinds with his paws. It's not a fox, it's not another dog, I tell myself. He's freaking out too bad and there's no way Ian would have just gone to get those guns if he wasn't thinking the same thing.

Ian thrusts the handgun at me, handle out. "Have you ever used one of these?"

Sweat trickles down my face and I shake my head. I take hold of the gun and it feels like a brick in my hand. I hold it at my side, pointed at the floor.

"I'm sure you won't need it," Ian says. "Just being safe. Keep it close until I get back." He takes a leash down from a coat rack next to the door and clips it onto Ollie's collar. "Like I said, it's probably just a fox or something."

He heads outside and I pace the living room, then go into the kitchen to get my phone. I stare at the screen, thinking about calling 911, but the whole point in coming here was to escape attention. I don't know what to do and I shove my phone into my pocket. I go back to the living room, the weight of the gun still dragging at my arm.

Suddenly, I realize it's quiet. At some point, Ollie stopped barking. I tell myself this is a good thing, that whatever it was probably ran off again. I walk to the window and part the mini-blinds, trying to look out. All I see is my own reflection. I step back and wait before going to the door again. I listen, my ear nearly pressed to the wood. I reach for the knob, my heart pounding as I crack the door open. Gray-blue eyes stare in at me.

I try to slam the door closed but his hand stays pressed against it, the act of keeping the door open seeming to cost him no effort. I expect him to shove it open, to rush into the room, but he doesn't. Instead, he keeps his eyes on mine. He speaks calmly.

"Autumn, we'd like to talk with you," he says. "Can we come in?"

It's too late, I can't close the door, so I jump back and raise the gun. "Who the hell are you? Where's Ian?'"

Gently, he swings the door open and I level the gun at his chest. He's tall, well over six feet. Behind him, I see a woman standing next to Ian. They both stare back at me, her expression unthreatening and Ian's blank.

It seems ridiculous, but I ask, "Where's Ollie? Where's the dog?'"

The man steps into the room now as I take another step back, the gun wavering between him and the woman. She must be the same one who'd been with him earlier and I expect the two of them to be monsters. That's not what I see. He's pale and thin, wearing a long dark coat left unbuttoned despite the chill of the night. She stands a head shorter, maybe in her forties, with wavy auburn hair showing streaks of gray. Amazingly, she offers a gentle, almost sympathetic, smile.

"The dog's fine," the man says. "He'll wake up soon."

I remember their swift attack upon the women who'd confronted me. He has to be lying; the dog must be dead. "What about Ian? What did you do to him?"

Even as I ask, something tells me that I already know. Rachel's words come back to me. *My eyes, they went funny. I saw lights.*

"He'll come around in a moment," the woman says. "We didn't want him to get hurt."

It's only now that I notice she holds Ian's rifle at her side, her arm relaxed, the barrel pointed down at the ground. I lower the gun that no longer seems to make any sense being in my hand. She could have shot me if she'd wanted to. I wouldn't have stood a chance.

"Thank you," the man says, glancing at the lowered pistol. "I'm Paul. This is Claudia. We came here to tell you what you are."

CHAPTER 18

Elliott knew as soon as his father invited him into his study My pulse continues to race even though I don't seem to be in any immediate danger. Still, how can I be sure? I have no idea what these people are about, but I certainly know what they're capable of doing.

"What do you mean?" I say. "Who are you?"

"It's rather complicated," Paul says. "Some of it, I suspect you'll have a hard time believing."

"You might be surprised."

They stand as any guests would upon entering your house. They glance around at their surroundings but keep their attention mainly on me. Except for Ian, who walks to the sofa, sits down and stares at the floor.

"How about I make some coffee?" Claudia raises her eyebrows. "We're sorry to have woken you up this way. There didn't seem to be a good time."

I stare at her, my mouth dropping open. "Coffee?"

She shrugs and offers a slight smile. "I could, if you like."

"I'll get it."

I spin at the sound of Ian's voice. He blinks back at me as if just waking up. "Where's Ollie?" he says.

"They said he's asleep."

Ian nods. "Right, that's true. I remember now."

"How is that possible? What did they do to you?"

Ian shakes his head. "I'm fine. They... they explained that they didn't come here to hurt us. That's about all I remember."

That in itself is terrifying to me, that they can control people somehow.

Paul's eyes meet mine again. "As Claudia explained, we wanted to be sure no one got hurt."

"Where's a good place for this?" Claudia holds up the rifle like she's asking where to put her umbrella.

"You can just leave it in the corner," Ian says. "I'll lock it up later." He gets up and shakes his head again. "I'll go make coffee."

My head swivels back and forth. "What the hell is going on?"

Paul hangs his coat on one of the hooks by the front door. "Let's go in the kitchen," he says.

"That sounds nice," Claudia says.

They follow after Ian and I follow them, momentarily speechless.

~~~

In something that feels like yet another bizarre dream, we sit at the kitchen table as coffee brews. Me, Ian and them, whatever they are. I keep looking back and forth between Paul and Claudia, waiting for one of them to speak.

"I've been wondering where to begin," Paul finally says. "And it seems that the best place is by asking you a question." He glances at Ian but, for the most part, directs

153

his attention to me. "Do you believe in non-physical entities?"

Involuntarily, I shake my head and then realize it's in complete contradiction to the truth. I'm not supposed to believe in such a thing but, of course, I do. And Paul knows this somehow, I feel sure. "You mean ghosts," I say.

Paul nods. "That would be a good example."

I hesitate but see no reason to lie. "Yes, I believe in ghosts."

"Okay, let's take it a step further. Do you believe it possible for there to be other kinds of sentient non-physical life?"

I'm not at all sure where he's going but, again, I get the distinct feeling he somehow knows at least some of what I've experienced. A chill rushes through me. "Such as people who've had their bodies taken," I say.

Again, Paul nods. "Yes, that's exactly what I mean."

I can't take it anymore, sitting across from him while he questions me. "Who the hell are you and what do you want?"

"Well, to simplify, we're beings who have the ability to inhabit a body that's not, technically speaking, our own."

"Jesus Christ!" I slide my chair back from the table, eyeing the gun I left on the counter. My gaze flicks to Ian, who stares wide-eyed.

Other than slightly lifting one hand, Paul doesn't move a muscle. "Please, be patient."

My focus shifts back and forth between him and Claudia. "What are you saying—did you take my sister? Where the hell is she?"

"We don't know," Claudia says, but her eyes tell me that she knows who I'm talking about.

"Please let me explain," Paul says. "As I said at the start, it's not an easy situation to comprehend. I'm sorry to keep asking questions, but please bear with me as I ask another. Do you believe in dimensions beyond this one?"

"Do you mean heaven, hell? Is that what you're talking about? And why do you keep asking me all the questions?"

Paul shifts his focus momentarily to Ian. "No offense, I hope."

Ian nods. He seems both fully conscious and numb with shock at what we're hearing. "None taken," he says.

"I think the coffee's ready," Claudia says. "Why don't I bring it to the table?"

She gets up and retrieves mugs from the cabinet. She brings those, along with the coffee pot, to the table. Evidently, she likes playing hostess when she's not snatching bodies.

"There's milk in the refrigerator," Ian says.

"Wonderful," Claudia says.

"I'm not speaking about heaven or hell," Paul resumes. "Actually, I can't speak to the existence of either. What I'm talking about are other physical dimensions where life also exists."

"Like a parallel universe," Ian suggests.

155

Paul shrugs, indicating not quite. "We too speculate on that possibility, but that would be a reflection of this dimension, just an alternate version.

"Who's *we*?" I say. "Let's get back to the part you mentioned before. About inhabiting a body that's not, *technically*, yours."

It amazes me when Paul winces slightly at my emphasis on the word 'technically.' For some reason, I didn't exactly expect compunction from him. "I mean my people," he says. "Others like us, although in that context I was referring to the place we left when we came here."

Suddenly, I realize what he means. "You're saying that the two of you are from another dimension?"

"Milk and sugar?" Claudia asks, and I realize she's talking to me. She's poured a mug of coffee for each of us.

"That would be great," I say.

Paul sighs. "Not only is it difficult to explain but, as far as I know, no one has ever had to before. To us, there's never been any need and it's always been for humans not to know."

"Humans?" I don't know why it surprises me. Clearly, they're not human.

"Yes, humans," Paul says. "That's what you call yourselves."

"And what do you call yourselves?"

"Vamanec P'yrin."

"What?"

"That's what the people from Vamanec P'yrinn call themselves."

"I don't understand. Is that a planet or something?" This is insane and, if it wasn't for the experiences I've had, I'd be slapping myself in the face to wake up.

"That's our world," Claudia says.

Ian perches forward. He frowns with confusion and speaks slowly. "Where is this place?"

"Here," Paul says. "Except in another dimension." He turns his attention back to me. "And Autumn is one of the people meant to keep us from coming to this one."

~~~

I listen, my mind reeling, as Paul continues to explain. If we're to believe him, he's from a race of beings inhabiting another dimension existing in the same place as our own. Theirs is only one of many such dimensions and these dimensions are like layers, wrapped around each other in rings. His people have a planet where we have a planet, although theirs—from what he tells us—looks vastly different from our own, having been populated long before ours and consisting almost entirely of cities so large that they start at one coastline and spread to the other. While we're unaware of these dimensions—outside of what would be considered the most wild, unfounded speculation—their civilization advanced to the point where they could not only detect the other dimensions, but also visit them.

"The means allowing for this would be vastly beyond your comprehension," Paul says. "Imagine it, if you will, as a mix of what you would call spiritual and scientific. The most fitting term to explain it in your existing vocabulary would be magic."

"Magic," Ian repeats.

Paul takes a sip of coffee. "Yes, but that word carries connotations of wizardry and fantasy for you, from your films, books and other forms of popular culture. As I said, it's the closest word you have."

"What does this have to do with people's bodies being taken?" I say. "I don't understand."

Paul and Claudia exchange glances, telling me we're getting to the crux of the matter. I think of what Paul said before, of no one ever having to explain it. Not to humans anyway.

"We've never crossed these dimensions physically. That's simply impossible. When we first started coming here, we existed purely as non-physical beings.

We could see and hear but not be seen or heard, except by very few." Paul's eyes linger on mine for a long moment. "Essentially we walked amongst what you would call ghosts and were visible only to realm watchers."

"What's a realm watcher?" I say, but something deep inside tells me that I already know.

"I'll explain shortly," Paul says. "When we first started crossing over to this dimension, the visits were considered exploratory. For purposes of research only. But then we discovered something."

I feel that chill in my blood again. I speak softly, as if thinking out loud. "You found that you could live in other people's bodies."

"Yes," Paul says. "The discovery was extremely controversial, to say the least. It also changed everything. You see, while your world was vastly more primitive and brutal than our own, some saw the trade as being worth it. Essentially, coming here offered something close to immortality."

"For how long do you...remain in the bodies?"

"Until we select another host," Paul says. "Typically, the former host is disposed of. It's less complicated that way."

"Oh, my God." My stomach lurches at the implications. "How long has this been going on?"

"A long time," Paul says. "Hundreds of years, in fact. And while your civilization has continued to advance in almost all ways, back then your species was, in some ways, more in tune. Humans knew there were other dimensions. They believed in magic, demons, spirits and monsters. Some of the most revered among you were those who demonstrated the ability of perceiving and interacting with these other elements. Long ago, it was accepted that these humans were themselves partly supernatural."

"Supernatural," I say, a chill rippling up my spine.

Paul keeps his eyes on mine. "Yes. They aged very slowly. They healed quickly when sick or injured. For a window of time within their lives, they couldn't die. It was said that they weren't yet allowed to cross the border they'd been sent to protect. They had different names in different cultures—shamans, veil witches, seers, sorcerers, mystics and psychopomps, to name a few."

For the first time, I can't help but chuckle. "What the hell is a psychopomp?"

Paul actually smiles in return. "One of your mythological figures, who also happen to exist in reality. A psychopomp is someone who can assist a non-physical being in crossing to another dimension. Typically, what's thought of as the afterlife. However, a psychopomp can also force a non-physical being to cross over as well, which is a significant distinction. At one time, there were many more of you. And your kind was the one thing we feared. Because, we learned, that when your kind forced us out we didn't return to our own dimension at all. We went someplace else entirely—to either that heaven or hell, possibly, the existence of which we cannot verify. Those dimensions, we haven't been able to detect any better than you."

"Why should we believe any of this?" I have the strongest urge to take hold of Ian's hand. I tell myself that it's because we're the same, he and I. Two humans sitting across from two beings who aren't.

"I can understand why you wouldn't," Paul says.

"In fact, that's exactly what most humans decided to do," Claudia says. "They decided to stop believing it. You entered ages of science and reason. Creatures like us were banished to the realm of imagination. Which, for us, was good."

"Very good," Paul says. "In fact, we couldn't have asked for anything better. When humans stopped believing in beings like us, there was less and less belief in, and need for, people like you. As I said before, we called your kind realm watchers because you could see and eject beings invisible to us that we, ironically, once shared a realm with."

I do a double-take on his last words. "Are you saying you can't see ghosts?"

"Not in this dimension, because we have no natural connection with this world. Nor can we see our own kind, not when they're in a non-physical state."

Ian hasn't spoken for a while, but now he speaks up, a dawn of realization showing in his eyes. "You mentioned creatures," he says. "Monsters that people once believed in."

"That's true, I did." Paul's expression suggests that he's been waiting for one of us to make the connection.

"Vamanec P'yrin," Ian says. "It sounds sort of like…" He shakes his head.

Paul raises his eyebrows. "Vampire?"

"That's what I was thinking, yes."

"We've been called that too," Paul says.

CHAPTER 19

A clattering at the kitchen door breaks the spell, as Ollie bounds through his flap and into the room. Something like reality resumes and I watch, expecting Ian's dog to bristle at Paul and Claudia. That doesn't happen. In fact, when Paul extends his hand, Ollie goes to him, although cautiously.

I watch, stunned from what Paul just said. He speaks softly to Ollie, his voice just above a whisper. "That's a good boy," he says, stroking Ollie's ear. Almost immediately, Ollie's anxious panting slows and his eyes start to close.

"You're not putting him to sleep again, are you?" Ian says.

Paul shakes his head. "No need. As you can see, he's fine with us being here now."

I can't believe Ian's worried about Ollie at this particular moment. "Wait," I say. "I think you need to explain more about the vampire part. I'm assuming you meant that figuratively."

"Regrettably, no," Paul says.

My head is spinning and I drag my hands through my hair, pulling it back. "This is insane! You're saying that you're actually vampires. Wait, you both just drank coffee."

"Most of us don't drink blood anymore."

"Most of us. Anymore."

"We share the same origins but true vampires are a different sect," Claudia says. "We split off from them long ago."

"We rarely interact nowadays," Paul says. "Although, it appears that may be changing. Either way, those you call vampires found a different way to survive, born from what was at first an addiction, but which eventually led to a mutation. On the other hand, most of us simply regarded humans as a lesser species, not entirely unlike how your kind regard cattle."

"That's comforting," I say.

Paul nods, briefly closing his eyes in a gesture of apology. "Over time, that view has slowly changed. In regions such as mine, we've long opted for what we consider a more respectful means of survival. Lately, however, we've reached an impasse with another faction who agrees more with the sentiments of our forebears. A philosophical dispute, if you will. One I'd like your help in resolving."

"Me? How the hell could I help make that happen? I'm just—" I stop there because, after the last few days, I'm not entirely sure.

"Things have started to change for you lately," Paul says. "We know this because we've felt it. What you do, the power you have, resonates with us because of your relationship with the border between this dimension and those beyond it. Think of it as shockwaves that only a select few can hear. We're among them but we're not alone, of course."

I have no doubt who he's talking about. "Who were those... people last night? The ones you killed."

"Well, we didn't truly kill them. That's not possible. And the problem is we don't know. We have our suspicions who they might work for but we can't be sure. Either way, it would appear that your reputation precedes you. This might be difficult to accept, Ms. Winters, but essentially you're an evolutionary throwback to a race of supernatural beings yourself. As was your sister, I suspect."

"What do you know about Cassie? Tell me now!"

Paul barely reacts to my outburst. In fact, he lowers his voice and speaks softly. "These things you've experienced lately. Your sister experienced them sooner. When she was a child, in fact."

My heart keeps pounding, but for some reason I feel my pulse starting to slow. "That's true," I say. "Some things happened back then. Things I'm only just remembering now."

Paul's voice grows even more soothing. "Of course. That's how they heard her."

"Heard her?"

"It's an expression. An approximation. But, yes, when a realm watcher becomes active, we know."

"Realm watcher." I look to be sure Ian's following everything. He continues petting Ollie, and it seems almost as if he's stopped listening.

"As I said before, we can't sense when others of our own kind are around. Which is why we often mark ourselves in a manner that allows us to know."

"The tattoos," I say.

"Exactly. Which is why I require your assistance. After all, I could be right next to them and not know if they chose not to show me."

"You mean that other faction you mentioned." My own words sound muffled, distant, like something heard in a dream.

"They've gotten reckless, causing us to be noticed again after all of this time. I'm not okay with that, and I want you to help me find someone. In fact, I want you to do more than find someone. I want you to eject that person from this dimension. The head of the snake, if you will."

I start to see lights, pulsing and flickering around me. I tell myself to keep my eyes on Paul's before I fade entirely. "If I can do what you say, why would I help you?"

Paul takes a last sip of his coffee, then sets down the mug. "Well, we can keep an eye on people close to you. Your mother, for example. Your niece and nephew. I believe you also have a friend expecting a baby."

Even through the fog starting to envelope me, I sense the implied threat. I fight to stay conscious. "You better leave them alone, asshole."

"And I will," Paul says. "Absolutely. In fact, I'll protect them. You have my word on this."

"Why would I trust you?"

Paul keeps his eyes on mine. Only now do I see that, even in the light of the kitchen, they've started to glow. "Because every word I told you is true," he says. "The sun will be up soon so we need to leave. But there's one more thing. I'm sorry, but you won't remember any of this in the morning."

CHAPTER 20

We stay at Ian's place for two days and it feels strange to be there with him, this guy that I didn't know at all a few days ago. But we both agree on a few things as we continue to assess the situation. Nothing has turned up in the news about the two people who attacked me so, if anyone knows who they were, then they're not letting on. Our best guess is that no identities have yet been discovered.

We also both feel that there's no reason to think that the police suspect I'm in any way involved. That aspect has remained consistent, that a person heard an altercation of some kind and called it in. Whoever it was obviously felt it safer to remain hidden. There's been no mention of what came before the slaying. All news outlets report the same thing. A cry was heard, police were called and bodies were discovered. Ian says, more than likely, the police tried to question witnesses from nearby buildings, but my not being home shouldn't have pinged anyone's radar. There's just no connection between me and what took place.

One thing is for sure. The women who accosted me are dead. It's also possible that I just happened to be there at the time of the hit, for in many ways that's just what it seems like, a very calculated and premeditated event. How else could it have taken place in a matter of seconds? In short, all of it could have been nothing more than a bizarre coincidence.

Ian has asked me a few times if I'm certain that those two women addressed me by name and, the fact is, I'm not entirely sure now. Shock, I guess, but some aspects of what happened remain hazy. Something tells me I could have imagined that part, my mind playing tricks on me in retrospect due to the very personal threat I felt at the time. Because of all this, we both suppose it possible that it could be entirely safe for me to go back to my apartment. The threat—even if it originally targeted me—has been removed. Still, it might be best to keep laying low and maybe swing by to get a few things and check on Louie. There's probably no harm in that since it seems unlikely anyone trying to hurt me has my apartment under twenty-four hour surveillance. That would be all but impossible with the police crawling all over the place.

All the same, despite a few awkward moments, I'd be lying to myself saying I've minded staying with Ian. It's quiet where he lives, pretty and relaxing. I feel safe. Also, it's the first time that I haven't felt alone in a long time. Sure, people have been there for me during that time. My mother, Zach and Ellen, and of course, Molly. But I've kept my distance from them for different reasons.

That afternoon, Ian gets a call. I try not to eavesdrop but I can tell it's important. My ears prick up as he says, "*really*" and then "seriously?" He thanks whoever it was and then turns his attention to me.

"Okay, that I didn't expect at all," he says. He doesn't leave me on the hook for long before adding, "That was Phillip."

"The tattoo guy?"

"Right, that Phillip. Sounds like he got a ping on that drawing you did. Who knew there were tattoo forums?"

I cock my head. "Seriously? Like Facebook groups?"

Ian shrugs. "I guess. Something like that anyway. Phillip said he put a pic online and someone actually got back to him about it."

I wish I could feel as intrigued as Ian looks, but I feel uneasy. I've managed to fool myself into thinking this respite could last but, of course, that's just been an illusion. I can't hide here forever. "Did he get the guy's information?"

"Woman," Ian says. "But, yeah. Apparently, she has a shop in the Fan, on Lombardy. Think we should go pay her a visit?"

"Not sure we really have a choice."

"It would be a shame to let Phillip's detective work go to waste."

What can I do but agree?

~~~

Unlike Phillip's one-man operation over at Inked In, Jenna's Body Art appears to employ multiple tattoo artists despite the singular proprietorship suggested by the name. No one sits behind the front counter as we enter and there appear to be three partitioned work areas. We wait for a minute but when Ian clears his throat— announcing our presence above the alternative rock emanating from speakers somewhere— a young Asian woman pops her head out from behind one of the partitions.

"Hey guys. Give me a sec, okay?"

A few minutes later she walks toward us, displaying a panorama of tattoos on both arms as well as the part of her chest exposed by her v-neck tee. Whoever she is, she definitely walks the walk. She's followed by the client she must have been working with, a girl about the same age as me when I acquired my dragonfly. I don't spot any gauze so I'm thinking this kid just got a tattoo like mine, meant for more intimate occasions. I feel a twinge of nostalgia thinking about Justin, his smile, those days learning the touch and smell of him as we started to become one.

The woman's voice snaps me out of it. "Remember what I said, now. No peeking for six hours. Wash but don't scrub. Okay?"

The girl pays for her new tattoo and heads out the door, giving a shy but slightly flirty glance at Ian on her way. So, that new tattoo might be open to multiple future viewings is the feeling I get. The other feeling I get, not one I'm ready to handle at all, is a slight twinge of jealousy. No, just no, I tell myself. There's no way it's been long enough yet. I'm just not going to let this—

"Hey, guys, I'm Jenna. What's going on?"

Ian introduces us and tells her why we came. He shows her a pic of my drawing on his phone to refresh her memory.

"The one Phil put on the forum," Jenna says. "He didn't say a whole lot, just whether anyone out there had seen it and that someone had met someone they wanted to meet again. See, isn't that cool?"

"Which part?" Ian says.

Jenna glances at him as if he's clueless. "That body art can talk to people that way. I mean, that's what you remembered about whoever it was, right? It made that person special to you."

"Actually, that was me," I say, just in case she ever talks to Phillip.

"Oh, got it. That makes total sense." Jenna doesn't say why, but I make a mental note to remind Ian later that his face just turned red.

"But you're right," I say, "It made her distinctive. I know it must seem weird but I didn't actually catch her name."

Jenna glances at my ring and her eyes meet mine again. "Not weird at all," she says. "I totally get it."

"I figured if I knew what it meant—the tattoo, I mean—that I might be able to track her down. Like, maybe if it's a vegan thing, I might be able to figure out where she shops. Or maybe it's just something she was into. Something like that. I don't know." Now it's my turn to blush. Not at the connotations of the scenario so much as the lame explanation. A vegan thing? Really?

Jenna takes another look at the pic on Ian's phone. "Not to be discouraging, but I've done this design a few times before. A guy came in asking for it just the other night. Maybe it's a trend."

Ian and I exchange eye contact. "A guy?" he says. "How old?

Jenna shrugs. "I don't know. Maybe twenty-five. Why?"

"I don't know," Ian says. "I mean, he might know Autumn's friend."

I feel something nagging at me. "How late do you guys stay open?"

Jenna turns her attention to me. "Eleven weeknights, twelve on weekends." She smiles. "We catch a lot of our business at night after everybody else is closed."

"Do you happen to remember if most of the people who've gotten this tattoo came in at night?"

Jenna thinks for a moment. "Now that you mention it, I think so. Hey, a girl came in for that design a few days ago. She looked about your age, actually. I don't know, maybe nineteen or twenty. When was that party you went to? Maybe it was her."

My heartbeat kicks up a notch. "Was she blonde?"

"Yeah, she was," Jenna says. "Was the girl you're looking for blonde?"

"Definitely."

One of the other tattoo artists comes out from behind a partition where, presumably, she's been working with a customer. She wanders over to where we're gathered at the desk.

"Hey, Yvonne," Jenna says. "This is Autumn and Ian."

Not surprisingly, Yvonne is also a walking collection of vibrant images, including a flock of birds taking flight up her neck toward the underside of her ear.

"What are you guys talking about?"

My pulse starts to slow again while Jenna explains what we're doing. I tell myself that just because a blonde girl came in for this same tattoo, it doesn't mean she was Rachel. She could have been anyone and all of this could still turn out to be nothing but a series of coincidences.

"You mean the one Phil posted?" Yvonne says. "You didn't show me that. What's it look like?"

Ian angles his phone so Yvonne can see. "It's kind of cool, isn't it?" she says. "Sort of, I don't know, cryptic. Is that the right word?"

"Definitely," Ian says.

"I was wondering what it might mean," I say.

Suddenly, Yvonne's eyes light up. "I know who has one of those! I always notice body art, you know? Kind of goes with the territory."

Ian and I both nod like we totally understand what that's like while we wait for her to continue. Thankfully, she does.

"There's a guy who works out where I do. I guess he'd probably know what it means. You'd think so, right?"

Before Ian pounces, I ask, "Do you know his name? Maybe I could talk to him."

"No, but he's there like every night. White guy, red hair, kind of buff. Anyway, I'll ask him the next time I see him."

I'm sure Ian is as tempted as me to keep pressing for more details but neither of us do. It's likely to punch more holes in our story. All we can really do is thank her.

Jenna gives me a sweet smile. "I sure hope you find your friend again."

A minute later, we head back to Ian's car. The wind has picked up and it's starting to drizzle as we walk through the fan district, the sidewalks no less crowded than usual because of the brisk weather as people check out the shops and restaurants in that popular part of town.

"I wish we had more to go on," I say, as we get into the car. "About the guy at her health club."

"Give me some credit." Ian says, cracking a smile. "I'm a psychic private investigator."

CHAPTER 21

Despite Ian insisting on driving around the block three times before I get out of his car, I make it into my apartment building without any bodies piling up on the street. Unfortunately, I only make it to the second landing before a door creaks open.

"Autumn? There you are. I've been wondering if something might have happened to you."

It seems like no apartment building would be complete without some version of Amelia Owens. And it makes sense, given the odds, that no matter where you live one of your neighbors would be a nervous old woman whose husband has passed away. Amelia always seemed nice enough from a distance, but the few times Justin and I tried talking to her we learned a little too much to end up liking her. The fact is, she's distrustful of anyone who isn't white, straight and at least relatively conservative in appearance. I've tried to remain sympathetic—she is old, scared and alone, after all—but I've also tried to keep my distance since my patience isn't what it once was.

I turn and offer a smile. "I'm fine, Amelia. How are you?"

I know what's coming and I tell myself not to blame her. This time, it's perfectly understandable.

"Terrible," she says. "Have you any idea what's been going on around here? People were murdered right outside in the street!"

I turn and surrender the steps I'd gained. "Yes, I know. It's horrible."

"I was worried sick about you," Amelia says, which I kind of doubt since we've spoken maybe four times since Justin and I rented the apartment.

"I'm sorry. I've been staying with my mother. She hasn't been feeling well."

Amelia doesn't seem to hear my explanation. "Right out in the street! In front of this very building. Two woman were murdered in cold blood."

I tell myself this could be an opportunity. Maybe's she's picked up on something that hasn't been in the news. "Does anyone know who they were?"

Unfortunately, Amelia shakes her head. "No! It's terrifying. It could have been me or you out there."

Tell me about it. "I'm sure it must have been very frightening. "Did they find out who might have done it?"

Amelia scowls. "No. The police in this town are perfectly useless. They couldn't find a killer if he walked up and bit them on the nose."

"Well, I'm sure they're trying."

"Not hard enough, obviously." Amelia scowls. "They say they don't even have any witnesses. How is that even possible with all the people living around here?"

"That's what I heard too. No one saw anything?"

"I heard someone in the building across the street saw a man. A tall man with blonde hair. At least that's what they're saying."

My mind goes back to that night, as it has a million times. To those moments when shadows converged and I stood frozen, as if in a fugue state. But there's something else nagging at me, like a dream that just slipped away and can't be recalled.

"Probably just a rumor."

Her voice comes from far away and I shake my head, trying to regain focus on Amelia. "Rumor?"

"About the man someone saw. God knows, there's been enough rumors going around. Now if the police would just do their jobs and arrest someone!"

I mumble my agreement and say something about having to check on my cat, still fighting to drag that dream back into daylight. As I climb the stairs, I briefly imagine gray-blue eyes before that dream sinks back into darkness.

~ ~ ~

Two hours later, there's still no sign of Louie, although his depleted food supply shows that he's definitely been coming and going. That, along with a few scattered feathers in the living room, suggests he brought a gift or two, but then changed his mind about leaving them when I remained a no-show. Louie's a generous roommate, but he's not wasteful.

I sort through the avalanche of junk mail, microwave some frozen lasagna and sit on the couch staring at my buckets of paint in the corner. I should get to work on refreshing this place. That was the plan, after all. It's either that or head out to Rory's, and I know perfectly well where that's going to lead me. Still, I can't seem to focus. My mind keeps going back to what Amelia said and, with that, come more vague feelings, this time of concern for the safety of people I know. As far as I can tell, the feelings makes no sense. Still, it's not like I'm going to ignore them.

I check in with Zach first, then Molly, who both report things to be just fine. I save calling my mother for last since, other than a few texts following the incident, I haven't spoken to her in a week. The funny thing was, she didn't know about the murders and didn't understand why I was texting to say that I was okay. She's made a habit of opting for fiction over reality, so she's way more likely to be aware of the latest bestsellers than what's happening in the news. Not that I blame her. After Cassie's disappearance, I'm sure she's had enough news coverage for one lifetime. Then I went and popped that bubble.

As a result, recent news is still very much on her mind. Despite my attempts at assuring her it was just a matter of proximity, her inner instincts seem to know better. "Still nothing on those murders," she says. "I checked this morning."

"I know, Mom. I was just talking to one of my neighbors. The police will figure it out, I'm sure."

Why I say that, I can't imagine and my comment is met with silence. No one knows better than her that the police don't always figure it out.

I try again. "I'm sure there's nothing to worry about."

But clearly she's been worrying. "There's something I should tell you," she says. "When you came by last week. I didn't tell you everything. I think you sensed that."

"Do you mean about Cassie?"

"And possibly about you, considering what you told me."

I wait as a few moments pass in silence. And it scares me, this feeling I get that she's compelled to tell me something as if she's doing so while there's still time. "Mom, what is it?"

"Do you remember your grandmother? Your father's mother, I mean."

"Sure. A little." The fact is, I remember more the idea of her than her as an actual person. She died when I was six.

"Adrianna was a nice woman. She used to dote over you and your sister when you were little."

"I remember," I say. And I do, but just in the hazy way we remember things from early childhood. I remember the glow of her smile, the warmth of her eyes and the way my nose would wrinkle up at the smell of her perfume. "Why do you mention her?"

Again, my mother hesitates. "Well, Adrianna didn't like to talk about it, but there was something about her mother that maybe you should know."

"My great-grandmother. I never met her, right?"

"No, you never met her. And most of this I found out through your father. He never met her either, by the way."

"Oh." While my father never mentioned his grandmother, that never really entered my mind. I just figured she was someone who'd passed away before I was born. It never occurred to me that he'd never met her.

"Evidently, there was something different about her."

Somehow, I know before she tells me but I still ask. "Different, how?"

"For one thing, she used to say that she could see people who'd died. I mean, I don't know but the story is that it started when she was young and got stronger as she grew older."

"She could see ghosts," I say. "Like Cassie."

"And like you, I suspect. You haven't said anything but has that been happening?"

I hesitate, then say, "Yes."

A moment passes and I imagine my mother closing her eyes, nodding at gaining confirmation of something she hoped not to be true. "Well, your great-grandmother—Sarah, I guess her name was—said she saw other things. Strange things, people she claimed came from other places and lived among us. Beings she said were neither human nor ghost. She said she could send them back to where they came from, that she had some sort of power."

I hear the distress in my mother's voice and I think about trying to distract her with some trivial thing to ground her back in the present day. But I can't, of course, as I remember that sphere of light expanding into a tunnel. And something not quite remembered, just a quick flash of gray-blue eyes appearing within my mind. "What did she say they were? Those other beings."

"All manner of things. Demons, vampires, werewolves. Your grandmother only told your father this just before she died. I guess she was ashamed. Everyone thought her mother was crazy."

A chill ripples across the back of my neck and part of me doesn't want to know any more. But something tells me that I need to know, that I have no choice. "Was there anything else she told people?"

"Yes," my mother says. "According to your grandmother, your great-grandmother said that this thing— this curse, this power—is in the blood. It's handed down. That it skips generations, that no one could say when, but it always comes back and always will. She said people like her were needed to protect the veil, whatever that means."

I hear a pounding in my ears, the thumping of my own heart nearly drowning out my mother's words. "What happened to her? Did Dad know?"

"They locked her up," my mother says. "Apparently, she kept trying to kill herself but couldn't manage to die. She died eventually, of course, but not until she was very old. Evidently, she kept saying the same thing over and over. Something about the veil keeper, that the veil keeper wouldn't let her cross over."

CHAPTER 22

Paul and Claudia walked a path alongside the river as rain continued to fall and wind whipped in off the water. Light from nearby towers rippled and glinted on the surface of the river's undulating flow.

"It's pretty, isn't it?" Claudia said.

It wasn't a rhetorical question. Not entirely. She'd known mostly this world, but some part of her no doubt remembered another, if just vaguely.

"Yes, it is," Paul said.

Thankfully, the visual aspects didn't fade although the rest became muted over time. Once, there had been the rest to go along with it, that explosion of sensations upon taking a new host, a seemingly endless spectrum of new experiences. These days, though, Paul could no longer abide the old ways. There were less repugnant ways to insure survival, although not without a great measure of compromise.

"I like our rainy walks," Claudia said. "Although, I still say you have a flair for the dramatic."

Paul laughed. "It does seem to be becoming a bit of a pattern."

"You're troubled or we wouldn't be out here."

Paul thought about that, knowing she was right. Still, he tried. "I suggest walks at other times."

Claudia nudged him with her shoulder. "You suggest going to movies or plays at other times. When there's something on your mind, it's cemeteries or paths through parks. It's fine. You wanted to talk about her, didn't you?"

"You've always had good instincts," Paul said.

They rounded a corner as a man approached walking his dog. The dog stared and sniffed while the man kept his head lowered and his hood drawn against the rain. Paul, Claudia and the man mumbled greetings as they passed each other. Only the dog looked twice.

"The reset isn't holding," Paul continued. "Not with her. Have you felt anything with him?"

"I would have mentioned it. But, no."

It was an, at times, inconvenient aspect of both mind-paralysis and reset that a bond with the other consciousness temporarily lingered. Typically, Paul barely noticed, but that hadn't been the case this time.

"I expected weeks, possibly months." Paul said. "Her development is farther along than I suspected."

"You said that might be the case but, still, you tried. Why did you?"

Paul glanced over at her in the darkness, seeing her as if it was midday. "We couldn't be sure she was ready. We still can't be sure."

"We should have occupied her," Claudia said. "It would have been the better option."

Paul knew she spoke only out of anger, and fear, an emotion with which they'd only recently regained familiarity. "More than likely, it was already too late. We discussed that possibility. Doing so would also contradict what we've decided."

"And yet we suspect they've done the very same thing."

"We suspect they've tried," Paul said. "We can't be sure they've succeeded."

"She was a child. How could they fail?"

"Realm watchers have abilities unlike other humans," Paul said. "Strengths and perspectives that set them significantly apart. You know that." Paul hated to remind her but he had no choice.

A few moments passed in silence, no doubt as Claudia thought back to a distant time. But there was no point in bringing it up now and she didn't. Instead, she said, "What about Autumn? She'll never trust you. She'll see us as being no different. Did you think about that?"

"The odds of her trusting me were slim to begin with. It's hard to imagine how she could let herself."

Understandably, Claudia fell silent. Paul well understood, since theirs was a shared inner conflict, one they once couldn't have imagined wrestling with. But the time they'd gained had also brought about changes within them. Not all of them, of course, which was at the heart of the problem.

Finally, she said, "So that's it, then?"

Paul reached for her hand, felt the warmth of it within his own. "When we decided to bring you here, it caused outrage. It had never been done before, nor ever since. They closed the bridge after that."

Claudia nodded, knowing it hadn't been an easy decision for them to make.

"We didn't feel that we had a choice," Paul said. "If, despite all the advances our people had achieved, they still couldn't save you, then we thought it a very small price to pay. Some called coming here unnatural, others exploitation and enslavement. We saw it only as a means for your survival."

Claudia spoke softly. "You sacrificed too much."

Paul didn't hesitate. "No, we didn't. Since that time, I've watched you grow and change. I've watched you bring about change, in others as well as myself. You were the one who convinced me that there was a difference between life and existence. That there was wrong in what we were doing, that we had no right anymore, indeed if we ever had. Have you changed your mind?"

Claudia squeezed his hand, a response completely human in nature, although she could barely know otherwise. She spoke softly. "No, I haven't."

"Good," Paul said, squeezing her hand as well. "I'm proud of you."

It was only after he said it that Paul realized it was a very human thing to say.

CHAPTER 23

"He goes by the name of Nathan Byrne," Ian says, driving us north through the city. "Although presumably that's an alias. He lives at two-twenty-three Vickerson Street, no known employment. He typically works out at Gold's Gym from roughly nine to ten-thirty each night. Not always weekends, but pretty much religiously on weeknights. Oh, and he drives a black 2016 Camaro, license plate VPRN221."

"I'm impressed, I have to say."

"Well, I did have some information to work with."

I pick up on the note of pride in Ian's voice, not that I blame him. "You had a rough description."

"Well, I also knew that Yvonne worked out somewhere as well as where she's employed. One thing led to another."

Out of habit, I scan the sidewalk to see if there might be any ghosts mixing in with the living. I think I spot one—a short, hunched over man reaching out to people who don't seem to see him—but we're moving too fast to be sure. "So, do we go talk to him?"

"Eventually, maybe," Ian says. "I was thinking that first it might be a better idea to follow him."

"Because one thing will lead to another?"

"With any luck."

A few minutes later, we pull into the parking lot behind the health club. The gym stays open twenty-four hours and, given the number of cars in the lot, it would appear that a fair amount of their clientele enjoy working out at night.

"Here comes the exciting part," Ian says.

"What's that?"

Ian looks over at me, his grin illuminated by the lights overhead. "We sit here and wait. Welcome to the exciting world of private investigation."

Given that it's just now going on eight-thirty, that's what we do for the next forty-five minutes. Sure enough, though, not long after that a black Camaro drives into the parking lot. Why I expected this guy to be flying under the radar, I don't know, but his muscle car rumbles loud and vibrates with the pounding bass of rap music. The music cuts off and we watch as a young man emerges, looking as Yvonne described, white with shortly cropped red hair. He wears a tank top and shorts, despite it being in the lower fifties outside. Even in the dark, you can see that this guy is cut from working out, his arms and legs bulging with muscle.

"Jesus," Ian says. "I sure hope things don't get physical."

I have to laugh. "Oh, come on. You were in the military. I bet you could take him."

"I was in the Army, not the X-Men."

Nathan Byrne disappears inside and our excitement is over for now. Part of me still wonders why we didn't just ask him about the tattoo. I guess that must mean I don't exactly have the temperament for the PI lifestyle. I'm already itching to get out of the car. At the same time, I'm sure Ian's instincts are sound. We'll probably learn more in the long run by just observing.

"Speaking of mutants," I say, "tell me a little more about that whole psychic thing you've got going on."

Ian chuckles. "What did you want to know?"

"You said it was in Iraq when you realized you couldn't ignore it anymore. But you mentioned getting feelings about things long before that. Did you mean when you were a kid?"

I'm thinking about Cassie, of course, wondering how much she might not have told me. Was it because she was afraid of being different? Or did she just assume it was the same for everyone?

"Definitely, when I was a kid," Ian says. "I just got feelings about things. Like one time, when I was seven, my family was out of town and I started getting super agitated. I told my parents to ask the neighbors to check on the house. They were supposed to feed the dog, let her in and out, that sort of thing while we were away. That's what my parents thought I was worried about. Which I was, but not in the way they were thinking."

"What was going on?"

"A fire," Ian says. "My mother left a space heater on and it was too close to a blanket."

"Wow. How did you know? I mean, did you see images or something?"

"I kept smelling smoke."

"Seriously?"

"Yeah, seriously. And from there I just sort of knew."

"Didn't that freak your parents out? You said you were just seven, right?"

"Right, but not really. I mean, a little, but they figured it for some sort of weird coincidence. Like maybe I'd noticed the space heater being on, something like that."

"Okay, I guess I can see that. It's not like anyone's first conclusion is going to be, 'Hey, our son has psychic powers!'"

Ian laughs. "Exactly. There were other times over the years, like when I knew my mother was going to have a car accident, or the time my sister was going to get hurt skiing. And it wasn't always bad stuff either. One time, I imagined us all getting on a plane and then my father came home and told us we were going to London that summer."

"And you ignored this happening to you," I say.

"Tried to. It seems strange now, looking back. It's like trying to pretend you're not gay, or smart, or double-jointed. You just are what you are. Some people have mad skills when it comes to math, and others when it comes to intuition. Same kind of thing, I guess. Then there were the auras I saw around people. How I managed to convince myself that–" Ian stops as if he just said something he regrets. He tries to recover. "Anyway, like I said, years later when I was in—"

"Hang on," I say, suddenly trusting a very definite feeling of my own. "What was that about auras? You totally self-censored there for some reason."

Still, Ian hesitates as he looks out at the parking lot. "It's probably nothing. It's just that sometimes I see auras. I get a sense of what people are about that way."

"How often does that happen?"

Again, he hesitates. "Pretty often."

The feeling I get is that he both wants to tell me something and, at the same time, doesn't know if he should. I'm a little afraid to ask, but I still do. "What is it?"

"Well, to be honest, I almost always see auras. The thing is, I've gotten so used to it that I barely notice unless I decide to tune in for some reason. On the other hand, there have been a few times when I've noticed someone not having one."

"When was that?"

"Well, it happened with someone when I was investigating what happened to Ryan McKenzie."

"The dead end guy," I say. "The guy who vanished without a trace."

"Right," Ian says. "It was someone who people said he'd been hanging around with before he went missing."

"When else did it happen?"

"It also happened when I found Emily Richards. That night I talked to her and she said that I must have mixed her up with someone else. Look, I'm sure it doesn't mean—"

"Any other times?"

Ian sighs through his nose, involuntarily signaling something between frustration and confusion. A few moments pass before he speaks. "You," he says. "I have no idea what it means, but you don't have one either."

~~~

Over an hour passes as we wait, which gives me plenty of time to mull over what it means not to have an aura. I want to think Ian is a combination of confused and just plain wrong, but the other things he told me about make me think he isn't. The fact is, he seems entirely plugged into that aspect of himself he tried so long to deny. For some reason, my skin is also crawling again with that same feeling from before when I talked to Amelia. It's like my brain is trying to make some connection between myself and what Ian said about encountering people who aren't exactly normal. I can feel it being there, whatever it is—a dream, a memory, or a combination of both. What the hell is it?

Once again, I imagine gray-blue eyes. I hear words inside my mind in a voice that I can't place. *Witch, shaman, seer.*

"There he is," Ian says.

I snap out of it as Nathan Byrne emerges from the club and swaggers across the parking lot again. It's grown even darker in the time that's passed, the light of the moon eclipsed by dense clouds that have rolled in across the sky.

I can't help it, I have to ask. "What about him. Does he have an aura?"

Ian reaches for the ignition, then leaves his hand resting there. "You sure you want to know?"

I go to shake my head, then nod instead. "Yes."

"Not that I can see."

And the words keep resonating within me. *Mystic, sorcerer, realm watcher.*

My eyes go wide at the last word, my pulse suddenly escalating. I turn to Ian, an unformed question on my lips.

"Seatbelt," he says, breaking my concentration. "You forgot to fasten it."

He starts the car and follows the Camaro, pulling out into Friday night traffic. Fifteen minutes later, Nathan Byrne parks down in Shockoe Bottom. He gets out, starts walking and we follow at a distance. We cross a cobblestone street when he disappears into an alley. I half expect the alley to offer nothing but dumpsters and darkened doorways, but we find a flashing neon arrow pointing us toward a flight of stairs. There, we find the entrance to a place called Fusion Hookah.

Inside we find a hazy den, where hanging rectangles of blue light cast an icy glow across the faces of a young clientele. I'd expected to encounter something sinister, but people sit gathered at low round tables as they talk and laugh, while drinking, eating and passing hookah hoses. Some sort of Middle Eastern flavored techno music pulses loud, and a quick check shows that it comes from an adjoining room with a packed dance floor and strobing lights.

Ian nudges my shoulder, and I follow his gaze to see our man cutting his way through that room and into a hall. We follow again to find that the hall leads to a labyrinth of other rooms. We pass spaces seemed intended for private dining, and people look up as we glance in. At the end of the hall, we spot Nathan just before he ducks into one of those rooms. We exchange glances and keep walking. We stop when we get to the doorway and we look in. Another group sits around a large table in a smoky, dimly lit space. I catch just a quick glimpse of the crowd in there, when our way is blocked by none other than the man we just followed.

"Private party, guys," he says.

Nathan's gaze flicks from me to Ian, then back to me. His eyes start to widen, as if with recognition. It makes no sense, but something tells me to hide my face. I pull my phone from my pocket and stare down at the screen. Within me, a surge of energy starts to spread. My skin tingles electric, like lightning is about to strike.

"Sorry, just looking around," Ian says. "Never been here before."

"Like I said, private party."

Ian clutches my arm and steers me back down the hall. "What just happened?"

"Not sure," I say. "Just... I don't know. Something." Even now, the warmth I felt spreading through me before keeps pulsing out from my solar plexus. As if something inside me just acted on instinct, knows something I don't consciously know.

We go back into the main room, claim a two-seater booth in the corner and Ian goes to the bar. He comes back with a glass of wine for me and a Coke for himself.

I take a sip of the wine. "What did you see in there?"

"A group of people, maybe ten or twelve," Ian says. "Everyone seemed pretty focused, almost like it was some sort of meeting."

"I'd love to know what that's about."

Ian nods. "Me too. I didn't see the woman doing the talking. Our buddy blocked the view before I got a chance."

"Should we get out of here?" I feel uneasy, to say the least. And I'm not sure how much more we can learn with him in there and us out here.

Ian sighs. "I thought about that, but I think we should stay."

Which is pretty much what I expected him to say. "How's your spidey sense on this one?"

"Richter scale seven."

Which is also what I expected him to say, since I have the same feeling. It's the other feeling I'm not sure how to handle. Even now, my body buzzes and I realize it's the same thing I felt when I brought Louie back to life. The same energy that coursed through me just before I crossed that ghost at the bus stop, and when I released the woman at Zach and Ellen's house. What is it and how can the same feeling be connected? Why the hell am I feeling it here? I take another sip of wine, but it doesn't seem to make much difference. Some spidey sense of my own has kicked in, like when Ian's dog somehow knew something was outside.

My head snaps up and I jolt in my seat. I stare at Ian. "The other night at your place. What was outside?"

Ian shakes his head, drawing a blank. "Sorry. Give me another hint."

"Ollie started barking at something. It was like—" I wrack my brain trying to remember the time but I don't. Part of me says it must have been a dream. "Three, maybe four in the morning?"

Ian thinks for a moment, his forehead creased as he tries to recall. "Sorry, I totally don't remember that."

Something else comes back to me. Something that can't possibly have happened. Still, I have to be sure. "You have guns, right? At the cabin. You got them out just in case."

Ian squints with thought, then shakes his head. "No way. I mean, I keep guns there but there's no way I'd forget. Besides, they're locked up. I always check before leaving."

So, it was a dream. It had to be. And it makes sense that I would have had bad dreams that night, given what happened earlier. It would have been a miracle not to have nightmares. A few minutes pass while I sip my wine and try to relax. I'm too keyed up about all of this, hoping to find out what happened to Cassie. So, we followed some guy with a tattoo to this place. Maybe we're grasping at straws. The tattoos, all of it, could mean anything. I need to calm down. At least for now, I need to let it go.

It's ridiculous but I realize that the song from the movie is going through my head. I think of how, just a few nights ago, I watched *Frozen* twice with my niece and nephew. I'm not even aware of the smile tugging at my lips until Ian notices. I tell him about visiting with Zelda and

Ethan, and how I've been meaning to be a better aunt to those kids.

"Try not to blame yourself," he says. "I'm sure it hasn't been easy."

Maybe it's part of being psychic, that he's sensitive to what people feel, but Ian's eyes tell me he knows exactly what the issue has been. And the fact is, I can't think of anyone better to share it with.

"It's just hard sometimes," I say.

Ian nods. "It's only natural that you might need to keep a little distance for a while. And it's okay. You've needed time to heal. The last thing you'd want is for your niece and nephew to pick up on the fact that it's painful for you to be around them."

I blink as my eyes start to fill. "Exactly. I think they might have known somehow."

Ian doesn't hesitate. "They would have, absolutely. Kids are remarkably intuitive. From what you're telling me, though, it sounds like you're starting to come around again. I'm sure your niece and nephew sensed that too. It sounds like the three of you had a great night together."

"We really did. It made me think—" I shake my head. "Never mind."

Ian's gaze remains on mine. "It's about your friend being pregnant, isn't it?"

I know I didn't tell him and, for a moment, I wonder if he might have found out when he investigated me. But even if he knew about Molly being my friend, he still couldn't know she was pregnant. I part my lips to speak but no words come out.

"I'm sorry, that was probably out of line," Ian says. "Sometimes, I don't know when not to say anything."

"How did you know?" It's a stupid question, based on what he's told me about himself.

Still, he just smiles. "You mentioned your friend the other night. When we were eating dinner."

I think back to the second night we were at the cabin. "I didn't think I said anything about—"

"You didn't. I just got a flash on it. A feeling." Ian shrugs. "Sorry, I know it can be intrusive sometimes."

"It's fine," I say. "I really haven't been able to talk about it with anyone. I just want Molly to know I'm happy for her. I mean, she gets it, of course. But the thing is, Justin and I weren't too far off from starting a family. We were thinking another year or two, at the most."

Ian glances down at the table, then back to me. "Which would have been about now."

"Right," I say. A silent moment passes between us. Not an awkward moment. Just the opposite. A moment during which we're both okay being around each other while thinking of someone else. "What about you? I know you were really young at the time, but you mentioned feeling that way about Shannon. That maybe the two of you could start a family someday. Has there…"

"Been anyone since?"

My face grows warm and I'm suddenly embarrassed at how personal the question is. "I'm sorry."

Ian offers a smile. "Not quite like that. I guess...." He shrugs again. "One of these days."

Without thinking about it, I place my hand on his. "Definitely," I say. "I bet it happens soon." I don't know if it's me making a prediction or just me wishing him a happy future. But in that moment, it just seems like it has to happen.

Suddenly, Ian looks past me to the back of the room. "That might be them."

I'm not sure if I should turn to look. I wait maybe three seconds, then look anyway and realize why Ian's staring past me. People emerge from the hall, all of them sleek, young and beautiful. They're striking, in fact—both genders, a spectrum of ethnicity, nearly impossible not to look at. They don't return gazes with those watching, exuding an indifferent confidence usually associated with celebrities. I realize that it makes no difference that I turned to look. They're not going to notice. Virtually everyone in the room has done the same thing.

My eyes go to a group of women, turned toward each other as they talk and laugh. One is Asian, her hair flowing down her shoulders like black silk. One black, walking with catlike grace, almond eyes and hair worn in natural wild ringlets. The other is white with shortly cropped platinum hair, the sides of her head shaved. My pulse kicks into overdrive when I see those now familiar symbols tattooed upon her neck. Just before they leave the restaurant, the blonde woman glances back. My heart jumps as I realize who she is. Visually altered, regal, thin and confident, the toned muscles of her arms and legs exposed in the shimmering dress she wears. Just her body language alone enough to render her nearly unrecognizable from the girl I've met twice now. But it's Rachel.

Ian grabs my arm. "That was her, right?"

I stare back at him, numb with shock. "That was her."

Others come out of the back and continue to walk past our booth. They disperse into the alley, the last to leave the same person we followed coming here.

Ian jumps from his seat and races outside, his instinct kicking in after what just happened. He's right. We might only have seconds before they're gone. I run out too, my heart pounding as I leap down the steps. I catch up and we stand where alley meets street. Ian calls out, his voice desperate. "Hey!"

I feel sure he won't, but Nathan stops on the sidewalk. He turns, car keys dangling on his finger. He waits as we draw closer. "Can I help you?"

"We wanted to ask you something," Ian says.

Nathan smirks. "Nothing too personal, I hope."

"Who were those people you were with?"

"Old friends. Why?"

Suddenly, I realize that the energy from before isn't just buzzing through me now. My skin burns, nerves crackling as if throwing off sparks. I step closer and raise my voice to be heard above traffic. "We saw her," I say. "That woman you were with. We know who she is."

Nathan shakes his head. "Honey, you have absolutely no idea who she—"

He stops as his gaze locks on mine. His eyes widen as he again makes some sort of connection. In that moment, I know. He's afraid. He steps back, further onto the sidewalk. He glances out at the street before locking his eyes on mine again. "Who are you? How did you find me?"

The roar of an approaching engine makes me raise my voice louder. "Where did Rachel go? Tell me where she went!"

He looks out at the street again, as if to be sure, then steps backwards off the curb just in time to be hit by the oncoming bus.

CHAPTER 24

Mayhem follows. The bus screeches to a stop, brakes squealing as the smell of burning rubber rises into the air. People scream and stare or look about in confusion. Twisted legs lay splayed beneath the bus. A dark puddle spreads, reflecting the glow of the streetlights above. People spill out of the bar to see what happened, some dialing their phones and others angling devices to film what just happened. In the distance, a siren wails.

Across the street, a woman looks at the scene as she gets into her car. She's young, like so many around us, somewhere in her twenties. Her eyes meet mine and she winks before closing her door. She starts her engine and drives off. I have no idea who she was or what kind of sickening urge motivated her to do that at a time like this.

I search the crowd around me and see that Ian has walked closer to the stopped bus and the people gathered there. He stoops to pick something up, then turns and walks toward me again. For the second time tonight, he takes hold of my arm and I'm glad when he does. I'm frozen until that point, unable to move.

He shows me the set of keys in his hand. "These were on the sidewalk. Come on. Let's go."

We start walking and it takes me a few seconds to come to my senses again. "How do you know those are his?"

"He was holding them at the time."

We get back to Ian's car and I drop into the passenger seat. Ian starts the engine.

"Shouldn't we give the keys to the police?"

"We could." Ian pulls away from the curb.

"Or?"

"There's bound to be an investigation, of course. But the only thing they'll be trying to determine is whether that was some sort of freak accident or a suicide. Chances are, at least a few people are likely to have seen what happened. Which means that, presumably, the police will be following up on a suicide."

I stare out at the road as he drives, thankful as the sounds of sirens fade behind us. "But that's what happened, right? He killed himself."

"Yes, and maybe no," Ian says.

I glance over at him. "Can you not be cryptic? I'm pretty freaked out right now."

He shakes his head. "I'm not trying to be cryptic. Just trying to put things together. We saw Rachel, right?"

"Definitely," I say. "That was her."

"But it also wasn't. We both know Rachel wasn't in that body. So, what I'm thinking is that maybe, for some reason, Nathan Byrne was afraid of you, but not the least bit worried about dying."

Suddenly, I see that woman getting into her car. The way she winked at me just before closing her door and driving off. "You think he left his body somehow."

Ian nods. "Which brings us back to that word again," he says. "Supernatural. I know it sounds crazy, but that's what I think."

I shake my head. "Not that crazy. Not at this point."

"Here's how I think it's going to go. They'll check up on the bus driver, of course. Anytime there's a pedestrian fatality involving public transportation, they'll have to check those boxes too."

I'm not entirely sure where he's going with this, but I have a pretty good idea. "Basically, a routine investigation."

"At best. A thousand dollars says they find next to nothing. Obviously, our man Nathan had some sort of identity going on. But I think they'll find he was a loner with no evident family connections or anything like that. But it's a suicide, not a murder, and there's only so much time in the day. It's not like they're going to run his picture in the news or anything like that. So, right, just a routine investigation and on to the next case."

"Great."

"Exactly. So, that leaves us two options that I can think of. We bail out or try to find out more."

Just when I felt my pulse starting to slow, it starts ratcheting up again. Yes, I need to know what the hell is going on if it can get me any closer to understanding what happened to my sister. Also, there's Rachel. If nothing else, I feel like I owe it to her now more than ever. If we don't figure it out, it's a pretty safe bet that no one else is going to. But that same thing keeps jabbing at the back of my mind, the feeling that there's some part of this I'm forgetting.

"What were you thinking?" I try to keep the fear from showing in my voice.

Ian turns briefly to glance over at me. "That we should check out Nathan Byrne's apartment. It's okay if you want me to drop you off at home. I completely understand."

I think about taking Ian up on his offer. At the same time, all I'd do is pace back and forth waiting to hear from him. "I'm in," I say. "Keep going."

~~~

The place turns out to be one of those upscale renovated warehouses down by the canals. Even in the dark, the apartment complex shows pristine. Ground-embedded sconce lights cast their glow across a smooth concrete walkway leading to river view apartments with balconies enticing you to bail on wherever you live, triple the cost, and never look back. Basically, it's one of those places that makes you sigh and wish whenever you pass by, thinking maybe someday but, realistically, probably not. Although, soon, someone is going to get lucky since it would appear that there's going to be a unit available.

It's getting late and, luckily, we encounter none of the residents as we enter the building. We take the elevator up and find the door displaying the number matching the address from Ian's investigation. Soon, we're inside and Ian closes the door behind us. He flicks on the lights to reveal an immense space with massive arched windows, granite counters, polished steel appliances and gleaming hardwood floors.

"I wonder what this guy did," I say.

"Just another one of my feelings," Ian says, "but I would guess nothing legal. Something tells me his crowd isn't exactly living paycheck to paycheck."

It feels strange speaking so dispassionately about someone dead less than an hour, and I have to remind myself that we're not talking about a regular person. Whatever we're dealing with, that much is for sure.

Ian glances over at me as if reading my thoughts. "We should just have a quick look around," he says.

We walk past the kitchen, into the main living area which turns out to be a total mess. Dirty clothes are strewn across the leather sofas and the chrome coffee table is barely visible beneath discarded food containers, empty cans, bottles and cardboard coffee cups.

"Who knew that a supernatural slob was a thing," Ian mutters.

"What are we looking for, exactly?"

"Not sure. Anything that looks...I don't know. Personal, I guess. To see if we can find out who this guy was. Any sort of evidence."

"And then what?"

Ian's eyes meet mine and he shakes his head. "Wish I knew. I'll go check the bedrooms. See if you spot anything out here."

Ian strides off and I'm not sure where to start. Despite all the crap in the room, there doesn't seem to be anything particularly personal. I go into the kitchen, opening drawers and hoping to find documents, letters, possibly even handwritten notes. I discover nothing but junk mail on the counter, dirty dishes in the sink and a refrigerator devoid of little more than condiments. Same for the dining area, where more laundry sits on the table, at least this time clean and in a basket, if hastily folded. I go into the bathroom, thinking maybe I'll find medications with labels telling us something, but again I find nothing. I keep searching, though, and realize that the buzzing has started within me again. That feeling like electricity races along my skin, the agitation building within me, but I don't know why.

I go back into the living room and pace the perimeter like a dog trying to pick up a scent. Something is close, I can sense it. My chest is heating up, my arms going from tingling to burning again. I don't know why but a thought shoots into my mind. *The clothes, check the clothes!* I dart back over to the sofa and plunge my hands into pockets. I find bills, coins, receipts for food, packs of gum and lint. I cross back to the coffee table, swiping aside cans and flipping pizza boxes to the floor. The table is clear by the time I stop. I pace back and forth, running my hand through my hair.

Suddenly, I stop, realizing that something other than my skin is buzzing. It's a phone, vibrating somewhere. Ian emerges from the hall. "There's a computer back there," he says, "but I don't—"

I hold my hand up and he stops. I dash toward the kitchen, my ears locked onto the sound. A brown leather jacket sits draped over a barstool at the counter. I lift it into the air and reach into the pocket. I take out the phone, thinking it has to be locked but it's not. It buzzes one more time and Rachel Joyner's altered image flashes onto the screen just before the attempted call ends. I hand Ian the phone.

"Yeah, that should do it," he says. "Nice work. We should go."

Ian's forehead shines with sweat as we walk toward the door. "You felt it too," I say. "Didn't you?"

"Not sure what you mean," Ian says.

He reaches for the doorknob a moment too late. The door slams back hard, throwing him into the room. She launches across the threshold, grabbing each of us by the throats and propelling us backwards. My feet spin as I try to regain traction, but I can't break free from her grasp. She hurls me backwards and I crash to the floor as she pins Ian against the wall. She turns to me and flips silky black hair from her face. "Wait there," she hisses. "I'll kill you in a moment. Do you hear me? Just stay where you are."

I stare back at her, lights pulsing around my eyes and a fog settling over my brain. My thoughts feel dulled and muted, as if I have a fever, but I know her from somewhere. Not somewhere, I realize. Tonight, just an hour or so ago. She walked next to Rachel on their way out of Fusion, that beautiful Asian woman.

She fixes her attention on Ian and his eyes bug as he tries to lunge forward. "Oh, sweetie," she says. "Relax, will ya? Take a deep breath and count to ten. Like, right now."

Ian takes a breath and starts counting, his body going slack. She keeps her hands clutching at his arms but turns back to me just as I'm picking myself up.

She smiles. "Uh-uh, naughty, naughty. You're a strong little bitch, aren't you? I said to take a chill pill, remember?" She narrows her eyes and cocks her head. "You hear me, right, honey? Nod if you can hear me."

The fog creeps in again, the flickering lights, like seeing stars but a thousand times more disorienting. I peer at her through the haze and nod.

"Much better. I'm Haley, by the way. Doing okay?"

"Doing good," I say.

"Great. So, something happened to my friend. You probably think of him as Nathan since that was his latest gig. Just like I'm Haley right now. You guys have the coolest names, by the way. What's yours?"

"Autumn Winters."

She tips her head back and laughs. "Seriously? That is too fucking beautiful. Okay if I use that down the road?"

I nod.

"Thanks. So, anyway. My boss called me and said she heard something from someone who thought he saw something and here I am. You know, to check up on things. But I'm outside getting out of my car and I hear you two prowling around up here. Do you have any idea how loud you are to us? Oh, my God, it took decades getting used to it but, you know, we adapt. It's kind of what we do."

She steps back from Ian and lets go. "How you doing? Doing okay?"

Ian stands right where she left him. "I'm fine," he says.

"Okay, good. Go sit on the couch over there."

I stare in shock as Ian walks calmly across the room to sit on the sofa, where he stares into space.

Haley sighs. "Where was I? Oh, right. So, I come over here because I kind of have to. Like I'm not right in the middle of watching Orphan Black. Hello? It's Thursday but, whatever, it's not like I didn't record it. Someone has to check up on Nathan because of the thing and it's not like Opal is going to take care of it herself. And I find you two here snooping, which tells me the thing probably happened." She turns back to Ian. "What were you looking for?"

"Evidence," Ian says. "We're trying to figure out what you people are."

Haley laughs again. "Right, good luck with that. Did you find anything?"

No, no, please don't, I think. Please don't—

"This." Ian takes the phone out of his pocket and holds it out to her.

Haley strides across the room and snatches the phone from Ian's hand. "Sweet, thanks." She thumbs at the screen and has a look. "Right, total Nathan move not to even have a lock on this thing. What a dipshit. Oh, look! There's a picture of us from last week. I look pretty hot, don't you think?"

Haley holds out the phone to show me a picture of the same people we saw tonight, clustered together for a group selfie shot. Nathan holds the phone as he squeezes in next to Rachel. Haley stands on Rachel's other side smiling at the camera.

Haley looks at the photo again. "Oh, too bad. Samantha's eyes are closed."

While she's been distracted by her own image, I feel the current running through me again. My mind clears as that charge builds in force. I act on instinct, pulling that power inward, imagining it as a blinding light growing within a closed black box inside my solar plexus. I pray that it works and that Haley's self-infatuation keeps her from feeling what's going on inside me.

Haley finally grows tired of looking at herself and turns back to Ian. "Here's the deal," she says. "I could just reset you two, and tell you to hit the road. You wouldn't even remember being here. But there's two problems with that. First, I don't know what brought you here to begin with so I can't possibly tell how far back you need to go. Obviously, you had an agenda. Second, I'm in kind of a crappy mood after getting called out when I was all chill in my jammies watching my show."

I keep my head lowered as that place within me continues to fill. I concentrate on that moment at the bus stop when I opened the rift, that tunnel, whatever the hell it was. *Keep talking, bitch,* I think. *Just keep talking.*

"So, what I'm thinking," Haley continues, maintaining her focus on Ian, "is that it's probably better to keep things simple. Ian, my good man, do you have any guns?"

"Yes," Ian says.

"Oh, awesome! Then do me a favor. After you leave here, take your girlfriend—wait, is she your girlfriend?"

"No."

"Do you like her? I mean, like, romantically."

Ian nods. "Yes."

"That's so sweet. You're cute, by the way. Or you used to be soon. Anyway, take her back to your place, or wherever you keep your guns. Once you get there, strangle her—knife's okay too, I really don't care—then shoot yourself. Cool with you?"

I wait, dreading Ian's reply, but he doesn't speak as some part of his brain still fights for control.

"Let me rephrase that," Haley says. "What are you going to do after you leave here?" She waits a few seconds, then snaps her fingers. "Ian?"

"Kill Autumn, then shoot myself," Ian says.

"Okay, good. Thank you." Haley shakes her head, as if impatient with a slow-learning child. She turns to me and does a double-take.

I stop advancing toward her when her gaze locks on mine.

Haley smiles. "Okay, Sunshine. Let's just get you to relax a little. How about you just—"

"Where is she?" The box within me bursts open, light spilling out. My body thrums, my chest heating up as the current courses down my arms.

Haley cocks her head and parts her lips to speak. She freezes with her mouth hanging open.

I push my arms out, spreading my hands, and the orb of light rises into the air. It hovers between us.

Haley's eyes widen and she steps back. "No way. You're *her*? You can't be... Opal said you were nowhere near—"

The orb expands. "Nowhere near what?"

She shakes her head, her body trembling. "I can't...she'll..."

I walk closer, my eyes boring into hers. "She felt it, didn't she? She knew about me."

Haley shakes her head again. "I don't know... I just..."

"Opal, right? She took Rachel, didn't she? Is that who you're talking about?"

Haley stands immobilized, and I'm not sure what has her more terrified, the force surging toward her from me or the thought of failing her boss. Either way, she doesn't have to answer the question. Within me, a door opens as the lock holding it closed finally breaks. Knowledge floods in, all those images and words returning to me. I see the two of them at the door to Ian's cabin, then coming in as I pointed the gun. I see the four of us sitting at the kitchen table, the incongruous sharing of coffee as I listen to words that make sense to me only in this moment.

Realm watcher. Evolutionary throwback. I hear my mother's words too, as she recounted those of a woman I'll never meet but who somehow imparted a message all the same. *This power is in the blood.*

"Here's what *you're* going to do," I say, taking another step closer. "You're going to tell me where she is."

Haley still hesitates and I spread my arms. The light expands even more, moving toward her. Somehow I know, all I have to do is push and she'll be gone. Sweat drips down her beautiful face as she stares.

I speak softly, forcefully. "Where the *fuck* is she?"

Haley's paralysis breaks and she nods repeatedly. "Okay, okay. Please, just don't. She's right here in town."

I speak through gritted teeth. "Be way more specific, bitch. And don't even think about telling me you don't know."

"No, no, it's fine. I know where she is. It's out by Wilton, a place called Lewis Cove. She has a house out there. It's on…it's on…shit, I forget. Wait! I remember— it's on Chandler Road. I don't know the address but you don't even need it. The place is huge, like a mansion, and there's nothing else around it. You seriously can't—"

From the corner of my eye, I see him stagger forward. "No, Ian wait!"

But it's too late.

Ian wraps his arms around her head and twists, breaking Haley's neck with a sickening crack. He lets go, steps back and Haley drops to the floor.

CHAPTER 25

I stare, horrified, my heart pounding. My entire body continues to vibrate as the energy, now with nowhere to go, lingers in the air around me like the pressure of a lightning storm. She lies twisted on the floor, her neck bent at an impossible angle, legs splayed and bloodshot eyes frozen wide in death.

I spin to face Ian. "You killed her!"

He shakes his head, as if my words make no sense. He speaks softly. "What was I supposed to do, let her kill you?"

He drops to one knee and turns the body onto its back. I force myself to watch as he searches her jacket pockets. He finds her phone and Nathan's.

I speak quietly now too. "I was about to cross her. I think. I mean, she couldn't do anything. I was..." I look down at my shaking hands, the energy withdrawing back into me now. My head is spinning and I feel like I might get sick.

Ian gets to his feet again, keeping his eyes on mine as he waits for me to continue.

"You don't remember," I say. "I understand. I'm not sure why I do."

Ian frowns. "Remember what?"

214

"Paul, Claudia. They came to your house. They told us what was going on."

"Autumn, I'm sorry. You're not making sense."

"Please, try to remember. You have to believe me."

"I want to believe you. I really do. These people, what else did they say?"

Maybe by telling him I can bring back what they somehow erased. "They said I was part of something that had been going on for a long time. He called me a realm watcher. That man, Paul. He said there were others who needed to be stopped, that they were different." I point down at the broken woman on the floor. "She's one of them. They took Rachel and they might have taken my sister. I don't know, they might have taken Shannon too."

Ian's expression shifts and he nods. "It's vague," he says. "I feel like I dreamed it, but I believe you." He glances down at the body again. "We can talk later, but we better get out of here."

I run my hand through my hair, trying to pull myself together. "What about her?"

"I don't see where there's any choice. We leave her and go. Now."

I have no doubt that he's right. It's not like we can report being attacked by a being inhabiting someone else's body, a person who also had incredible strength and could somehow control our minds. We'd be locked away and never again see daylight.

At the same time, it occurs to me that this person on the floor was once someone else entirely—someone's

215

missing daughter or sister. At least her murder will shine a media spotlight on the other death from earlier tonight, causing speculation that this was some sort of murder-suicide. Photos will be in the news, someone might recognize the people they lost.

I expect Ian to suggest using the stairs to avoid being seen but he doesn't. If we're seen leaving that way, he says, it will be remembered. Although, given the hour and the fact that a body is soon to be discovered, I'm not so sure we'll be forgotten if seen taking the elevator either. The time works in our favor, though, and we encounter no one as we make our way out of the building.

Ian unlocks his car and I hesitate before getting in. On one level it makes no sense. Ian killed Haley trying to defend me. Whatever Haley was—a being from another dimension, an alien, possibly a vampire—she's also not dead. She's just gone and it's only a matter of time before she takes another body if she hasn't already. That someone else entirely is dead, I can barely bring myself to think about. At the same time, I'm getting into the car with someone capable of snapping a person's neck.

Still, I get in and close the door. What else can I do? Ian starts the engine and drives forward, somehow calm even after what we just experienced. Of course, he picked up on my emotional confusion, and he speaks to that when he reaches the first red light.

"I'm not exactly comfortable with what just happened either," he says. "When I snapped out of that fog she put me in, and I saw the two of you facing off, instinct just sort of kicked in."

I nod, only now realizing that my eyes have filled. Stress, fear, sadness, confusion—all of that and more washes over me. "Was it something you learned in Iraq? To do that?"

"Hand to hand combat is part of military training," Ian says. "She was going to kill us. You know that, right?"

"Yes." I'm sure he's right. She would have killed us without another thought. Worse, actually, since she would have had Ian kill me and then himself.

"For the record, I've never killed anyone before. Not even in Iraq."

"I'm sorry," I say, hearing the pain in his voice and realizing that I've only been considering my own experience. We both have to live with the horror that just took place.

Minutes pass as Ian continues to drive across town. It's starting to rain and I watch droplets trickle down the passenger-side window, catching the light of passing cars and streetlights overhead. In the distance, the sound of a siren rises into the night and I wonder if it comes from an ambulance or police car racing toward the apartment we just left.

"Haley mentioned someone named Opal," I say. "I think that's her boss. She might even be the one Paul told us about. I know you don't remember, but he referred to her as the head of the snake. I think she might also be the one who took Rachel."

I've felt edgy since we left the apartment, that force within me still simmering close to the surface. As if those instincts, which kicked in automatically before, don't know how to shut themselves off again. I keep waiting for the feeling to dissipate.

"It's strange," Ian says. "I was so disoriented...it feels almost like none of that happened before. Those people in the bar, seeing Rachel. All of it."

He speaks softly. His voice, combined with the motion of the car, somehow lulling me. Despite everything— including my conflicted feelings over his admission of liking me romantically—I feel comforted now to be with him. He protected me, after all, was willing to risk his life doing so. Pulsing lights dance at the corners of my vision.

Ian glances over at me. "We'll get through this," he says. "Everything will work out okay in the end. I can feel it."

I want to tell him that we need to go to that house Haley told me about. If not tonight, then first thing in the morning. But my eyes are starting to close. Still, as we approach the intersection at Main and Belvidere, I notice that Ian's not slowing down for the red light. Even then, my words come out little more than a whispered slur. "Ian, the light."

He doesn't react to the sound of my voice.

I try to sit up. "Ian, the light!"

The world explodes in a combination of blinding headlights, screeching brakes and the deafening moment of impact. Then comes the pain, too overwhelming to even feel. My body feels numb, quivering and distant in the moments of shock following the crash. I loll my head to the window where I'd just been watching rain, to see a spider web mass of fissures that drips now with blood. My blood. I feel it too, warm and viscous, running down my face as I turn to Ian.

His eyes glow back at me against the headlight glare of that other vehicle still pinned to ours. The stink of burnt rubber, car exhaust and gas fumes rise to my nose. I want to think it's a nightmare, that I'm already unconscious, but I know that's not true.

"So, you're the realm watcher," he says. "How's that working out for you?"

The tears I managed to hold back before now fall from my eyes, mixing with the blood and running down my cheeks.

"God, you people are so slow," he says. "You really didn't figure it out yet?"

I shake my head, or at least I think I do. I can't tell because I can't feel anything. Whatever hit us—truck or car, I can't be sure—rammed into my side of the car and broke me. I look past Ian to see rain drizzling down the window. It reflects the streetlights overhead. My eyes stay on the liquid light as he starts talking again.

"Yeah, well. It's not like I didn't know that," he says. "You were like, *Oh, Ian, did you ever kill someone before? Did you learn that in Iraq? Sweetie, baby, honey, you're so scary to me now.* Give me a freaking break. First of all, do you eat meat? Tell me, where's the difference between one of you and a chicken? What are you all worried about killing for? It's so freaking hypocritical. But I can see that I'm losing you. So, my point is he snapped my neck because I made him do it, dipshit. God, I can't believe I missed Orphan Black for this crap. I'm seriously going to give Opal a fucking piece of my mind."

"Where's Ian?" I speak faintly, my words slurred.

"Seriously? In the fucking junkyard somewhere. Why should I care? So, are you dying yet? I heard that your kind was a total pain in the ass to kill. Then again, I also heard that your kind didn't actually exist anymore."

I keep my eyes on the liquid light and I think of my sister, my parents, my childhood. I draw the warm glow of the past in and hold onto it while, in the distance, I hear the wail of sirens.

Ian unbuckles his seatbelt. "Well, obviously, I need to get moving." It's Ian's voice but not his voice. And I know it's the last voice I'm going to hear. "So, yeah, let's get this done."

Hands clamp against my neck and begin to squeeze. The last thing I see before everything goes black is someone who looks just like Ian staring into my eyes.

CHAPTER 26

In the dream, I travel through a tunnel toward light and I know, once I get there, that everything will be okay. It's an entrance, of course, a portal to some other place much different from the one we know. It's where we come from and where we go back to each time. I know that, on the other side of that light, people wait—people I've known before and people I'll know again in some different future. It's a comforting glow, a fireplace in winter, a porch light left on at night, the flicker of fireflies in your backyard. It's home.

I travel toward it, not walking this time, not holding anyone's hand. I just move, I float, leaving the broken parts behind. I'm almost there when I see her eyes. Her eyes are all I have to see to feel the weight of her sorrow at what she has to say. "I'm sorry. You have to go back."

CHAPTER 27

The body throbs and you hear that first. Not the beeping of machines or the voices around you. Those come after. First, you hear the orchestra of pain shattering the silence. The last thing I see before opening my eyes again is Justin's smile. I see his eyes and I hear his voice.

I really want this for you. What do you think, babe?

I wake up thinking about Ian. The lost Ian. I hear the machines, monitoring, clicking and beeping. I hear the voices, a mix of male and female.

"Broken spine, fractured skull, shattered femur, ruptured spleen and internal hemorrhaging. That was five days ago, right?"

It's a man's voice. He sounds both angry and confused. A long pause follows before a woman speaks. She sounds young.

"The record speaks for itself," she says. "We can't explain it."

"Yeah, I get that," the man says. "No one could, because, obviously, someone mixed the files up." He pauses, then says, "Yes, I know. It's all in the digital file too. Which tells me that we have a major fuckup going on with scanning and indexing. Or, we got hacked, but there's zero indication of that since, obviously, there'd be panic on the streets while it's business as usual." Another pause. "This isn't a joke, right? Payback for what I did while you guys were interns?"

"I swear," the woman says.

"Holy shit," the man says. "What the hell is she made of?"

I'm too sedated to speak to this man standing over me. I feel weighted down and helpless within my own body, trapped within something broken. He continues to speculate aloud. Within me, a sensation starts to build, one that's grown almost familiar. My veins course with the sharp buzz of energy. My nerves tingle and heat rises within my chest. A moment later, I look down upon a bruised and bandaged, dark-haired young woman. She lies in a hospital bed. She's thin and pale, her eyes closed but her lips slightly parted as she breathes in and out.

I gasp and step back, the bright lights of the room suddenly spinning. Two people look back at me, a fair-skinned woman and a man with olive complexion. Their brows furrow with concern and I turn away. I walk to the window and gaze down three stories to the parking lot below. My hand presses against the wall, large with the slender fingers of a surgeon.

"Doctor Henning, are you okay?"

Get out, I think. *Get out now!* I imagine myself letting go, falling back through darkness. I feel the throbbing of my pain again as I take a deep breath. I listen to his confused response from where he stands now across the room.

"I... I'm not sure what just happened. I just..."

"You're pale," the woman says.

"I just felt lightheaded for a moment," he says, regaining control. "I'm okay now."

Even in my numbed state, I hear his uncertainty, the jolt of fear lingering in his voice. Another moment passes before he says, "Here, let me take a look at her chart again. There has to be some sort of mistake."

CHAPTER 28

The sun is setting as I pull into the rutted road leading to Ian's cabin. I find the key where he told me it would be if I ever needed it, hanging from a nail beneath the back deck stairs. I let myself in through the kitchen door to find the house still, the air within it stale. I wait another moment, half-expecting Ollie to come trotting down the hall but that doesn't happen. Someone from Ian's family must have come and taken him to look after while the search continues.

I've kept hoping that Ian came here, like Rachel returning home. I pray that, this one time, I encounter a specter even as I fear what that will involve. Still, I need to speak to him. I need his help and I need to find a way to help him.

"Ian? It's me. I'm sorry it took so long but I was in the hospital." I wait, looking around. An old clock I didn't notice before ticks where it hangs on the wall. "Three weeks," I say. "Can you believe that? But they said I should have died so I guess three weeks isn't bad. As you can imagine, they were a little confused."

I cross from the kitchen into the living room, and I stand in that space where curtains have been left closed.

"I figured maybe I'd come here," I say. "Do you mind? I wasn't sure if I needed someplace where I wouldn't endanger anyone. At least until I figure things out." Wind rustles through the trees outside. The screen door creaks against the breeze.

After a few seconds, I walk down the hall toward the bedrooms and stand where their doors face each other. "Your friend came to see me. Steve. He wanted to know what happened. I told him I didn't remember anything, but I don't think he believed me."

If anything, the house seems even more silent than before, darker now that I'm away from the front windows. I go back into the living room, knowing the truth. The same truth I knew while coming here but wouldn't let myself accept.

"Ian, goddammit! I need you. Where the hell are you?"

It's only when I break down that I realize the other reason I came here. If even Louie was with me, I'd find a way to restrain myself. The tears keep coming as I gasp for air. I look up at the ceiling and scream, "Goddamn you too! Why do you keep throwing me back, you bastard? What the hell do you want from me? Fight your own fucking battles. Come on down here and do it yourself!" There's only one other person I can think of to be furious with so I include Paul in my rant too. "Listen up, you albino beanpole! You can hear magic, right? Isn't that what you said? Then, pay attention, asshole! Because you and me need to talk!"

I don't even have to try because that current is already coursing through me, lighting up my veins, burning against my heart like a furnace and sparking down the skin of my arms. I open the rift, the portal, the tunnel—whatever the hell that thing is—and I keep opening it over and over until I'm nearly blinded by the brilliance of the light pulsing back at me. I have no soul to force through that opening, no ghost to cross, no purpose at all other than being more seriously pissed off than I've ever been before. And the fact is, I don't even give a shit when, on the other side of that thing, a group of hazy figures gathers to look back at me. Whatever, assholes. Don't worry about not inviting me to your party. I plan to have one of my own.

~~~

An hour later, I sit at the kitchen table with the bottle of bourbon and a Virginia Is For Lovers shot glass, which I've filled several times. Right now, it's empty so I fill it again. For Ian's sake, I also made tea and left a mug sitting across from me. Who knows? Maybe if our mission won't persuade him to show himself then a cup of Earl Grey will.

My rage is spent for now and I have another idea. Of course, that could be the alcohol, which could also mean it's not such a great idea. Still, I close my eyes and breathe deeply, evenly, knowing this isn't about that other energy. That pushes out, it's very essence one of disruption, causing something to fracture and open. Tonight, especially, it felt that way. Like I was kicking down a door. This other feeling requires peace and centeredness. I have to draw her toward me.

When Rachel appears, she's barely there. I feel her more than see her and it takes a few moments for my eyes to lock onto the space where she stands. She's little more than a silhouette this time, softly glowing at the edges and almost entirely transparent. Her eyes, though, I see. They stare into mine, searching and lost.

"Do you remember me?" Something within me tells me to start there, to go gently.

My voice calls her forth more. She flickers more into being in the space we share. She wears no clothes now, instead standing naked, although only her shape indicates a remaining connection with gender. She's past the point of imagining herself still living.

After a moment, Rachel nods. "From before," she says.

"Yes, from before." I didn't call her here to upset her, to bring her pain unless I can also offer deliverance. Something inside tells me I can make good on that promise, even if she's the only one I can save. "Do you remember what happened that first time we met? What you told me?"

It takes a moment but she grows less translucent, as if filling in with vapor to appear more solidly human. She flickers closer. "When I died? That's when I saw you. On the night I died."

I hesitate, weighing what's truly best for her at this point. "On the night when you crossed over to where you are now," I say.

Her eyes peer into mine. "The gray place."

I shake my head involuntarily. "Can you tell me about it?"

"We can wander or we can go to the gray place," she says. "The gray place is like sleep. It's quiet there and I don't have to wake up, not if I don't want to."

I want to ask her more, wondering if that might be where Cassie has gone, or Ian. But she's started to fade again, as if thinking of that place where she goes to find peace is enough to draw her away once more. Part of me wonders if it's more merciful to let her slip away, but I'm not sure I'll be able to draw her forth again.

"You told me about some people. They came to where you worked," I say. "Do you remember them?"

The effect on her is startling, something I've never seen. Her entire being flashes with emotion. The vapor filling her silhouette becomes a twisting storm before, suddenly, she stands before me as I first saw her—a young woman wearing jeans and a hoodie, her long blonde hair tied back into a ponytail.

She flickers back, abruptly jolting away from me. "No, I don't want to remember them!"

"I know. I'm sorry. I really am. But do you remember what you told me they did?"

Her eyes widen and she shakes her head in denial. "It's not possible. What I thought they did isn't possible! Please let me go back to the gray place. Why did you make me come here?"

I fight the urge to step toward her, afraid I'll scare her away. "What if I could get you home again? You won't have to stay in the gray place. You could be with your family, with your friends."

"No, I can't be with them anymore. I'm dead!"

"No, you're not. Rachel, you're not."

Her tears come and once again I marvel at that aspect—that pain or sadness felt intensely enough will find a way to manifest even in those no longer physical.

My idea from before returns to me, the reason I called her here. "Do you have any brothers or sisters?"

"A brother," Rachel says. "I had—I have a brother. He's a year older than me."

"I bet you guys shared a lot of secrets when you were kids," I say. "Am I right?"

For the first time, a soft smile tugs at the corners of her mouth.

"My sister and I had secrets too," I say. "If I tell you something, will you promise not to tell anyone else?"

Rachel hesitates, then nods. "A secret?"

"Between me and you. I need for you to remember it, okay?" When I step toward her this time, I don't worry about scaring her away. In this moment, Rachel knows she's still alive.

~~~

After that, I bail on the bourbon, sliding Ian's unclaimed tea to my side of the table. It's long gone cold but it still tastes good. Ian doesn't mess around when it comes to buying quality tea. I remain sitting in the kitchen, ruminating on the fact that I essentially just had a bonding moment with a bodiless entity preceded by throwing some sort of supernatural tantrum. And that both seem somehow within the realm of normal for me now. I'm actually chuckling when I hear the sound of an engine approaching.

I jump to my feet, looking for my keys, but realize it's already too late. The road is too far off so, if I can hear the car, it must already be on the property. I dash down the hall to Ian's bedroom and slide open the closet door. There's a gun cabinet at the back, a metal box hunkered against the wall. But it's locked, of course, and I don't know the combination. Then again, what good would a gun do? If it's a neighbor or friend of the family coming to check on the house, it's not like I'm going to stick a gun in their face. If it's Haley or Nathan or anyone from Opal's little cult, shooting them wouldn't make any difference.

In the living room, I peek through the curtains just in time to see a car come to stop. A Mercedes, not exactly a car suited to the rustic environment so this is probably not a neighbor or friend of the family. A tall man gets out and the moonlight reflects off of his silvery-blonde hair and the planes of his thin, angled face. My heart pounds as he walks toward the house, this being who I both know I've met and have kept thinking had to be part of some ongoing delusion. A moment later, the doorbell rings and I can't help it. Maybe I'm going insane, but I let out a stifled, nervous laugh.

I don't know what I expected—the door to be pulled from its hinges, a loud, insistent rapping, the terrifying moment of eyes peering back at me through a darkened window—but it definitely wasn't for him to politely ring the doorbell and stand waiting on the porch. I imagine him looking about and whistling and I check to see that he's doing exactly that, his face partly raised to the moonlit sky. What else can I do but open the door?

"I gathered you were trying to gain my attention," he says, entering the room.

Paul closes the door behind himself and the moment of laughter from before seems a total disconnect now. For all I know, he came here to end me. Part of me doesn't even care. It's been a long, rough year. "Well, you didn't think to leave me your phone number," I say. "Oh, right. I wasn't supposed to remember meeting you."

He shrugs, seeming almost embarrassed. "Well, not quite this soon anyway. Originally, I'd imagined reintroducing myself."

I shake my head, incredulous. "Why did you even wipe my mind to begin with? Oh, I mean 'reset' me or whatever the hell it is that you guys call it."

He slips out of his long coat and drapes it over his arm. It didn't occur to me before, but there's something stiff and formal about the way he holds himself. As if he hasn't been able to entirely abandon mannerisms learned in a different time.

"I'll do my best to explain," Paul says. "Should we perhaps sit down?"

I gesture toward the kitchen, thinking of Claudia hospitably making us coffee. "Sure, how about I make us a cup of tea?"

"That would be nice," Paul says. "Thank you."

The absurdity is nearly overwhelming. The man could strip my mind away, literally possess my body, quite possibly tear me apart with his bare hands, based on the display I witnessed in front of my apartment. But he rings the doorbell and whistles silently, drapes his coat over his arm like he's at the opera and responds with crisp politeness to the offer of tea. All the same, we go into the kitchen, I fill the kettle and we sit at the table.

"Just to clear the air," I say, "you didn't come here to kill me or anything like that."

Paul quirks his eyebrows, almost smiles. "I came because you called, essentially. By the way, that was less than prudent."

I heave out a sigh. "At the time, I didn't care. Why do you suppose you came and not them?"

"I can't entirely rule out that they won't." Paul glances at the stove, where the kettle has started to rumble. "At the same time, they haven't come after you yet. Which could mean any number of things, most likely one of two. Either they think you're too afraid and confused, most likely questioning your sanity. As I mentioned before, knowing what you know overwhelms the uninitiated mind. Quite often, this leads to being institutionalized. Equally often, to taking of one's own life. At least, eventually."

I think of my great-grandmother, Sarah. It's frightening to realize that one of their most reliable defenses is to let us take care of the problem ourselves. Basically we go crazy and either get locked away or commit suicide as soon as we can. I force myself to keep my eyes on his. "What's the other possibility?"

Paul shrugs. "That they're afraid."

My eyebrows shoot up. "Of me?"

He nods. "Mortality is a truly terrifying concept for anyone, but much more so for those who've known centuries of life. Add to that, as far as we know, you're the only person who can actually kill them."

"Holy shit," I say, as the kettle shrieks behind me.

"Indeed," Paul says, but he frowns slightly and I get the feeling that my language offended him.

~~~

I try to process what Paul just said as I make the tea. It's getting late so I choose decaf this time, not thinking to ask what he'd prefer. Something tells me that caffeine, or the lack of it, isn't exactly a concern when dealing with body-jumping supernatural beings. I bring the tea to the table and sit across from him again.

"Why wouldn't they just kill me from a distance? Easily achieved with a gun and they don't even have to worry about being caught. Not really."

This time, Paul allows a slight smile to play on this lips. "Is it safe to assume that the hospital staff was once again puzzled by your condition?"

Despite the weeks that have just passed, part of me has kept wondering if it could really be possible. "Wait. You're saying it's literally true?"

Paul nods. "As far as we've been able to observe. And it's important to understand that, while we have our allegiances, our loyalty only goes so far when it comes to actually facing death."

I pour tea into each of our mugs. I almost feel like it's tempting fate to ask, but I'm not sure when I'll have another chance. "Why not just mesmerize me—you know, that thing you guys do—and take over my body?"

Paul draws his mug closer. "As you grow stronger, you also gain resistance to mind-paralysis. Which isn't to say you're impervious. No one is. All the same, both eviction and occupation require it as well as a certain measure of proximity. Both would require too much risk at this point."

"I'm assuming you know they took Ian," I say.

"We knew you two were in a car accident. We know that Ian's since gone missing. From there, it wasn't hard putting the pieces together."

"I keep thinking he must be dead."

Paul doesn't hesitate. "But you know he's not. You can feel it somehow."

It feels true, what he's saying. Just like I tell myself that I somehow know with Cassie. I nod and say, "I hope you're right."

Paul raises his eyebrows, as if to say *Don't be so sure.* "I should explain more than time allowed for the other night. I'm sorry, but it's a lot to comprehend." He blows at his tea and takes a sip, the act so normal. So human. "As you know, we can evict the consciousness of the host we choose. However, we can also choose to occupy."

My stomach twists as his meaning sinks in. I take a deep, sudden breath. "Oh, my God. Are you saying what I think you're saying?"

"It's not a choice we make often. The fact is, the condition is just too unpleasant. But you should know that, in those instances, you'd risk ejecting the consciousness of both from this dimension when attempting to eject one. They become somewhat...intertwined."

Despite everything I've learned so far, this revelation is the most appalling, literally sickening to consider. I take another breath, fighting a wave a nausea. "Is that what happened to my sister? And to Ian?"

Paul shakes his head. "I simply don't know, but it's possible."

My mind reels and a dangerous anger flares inside me. Paul seems to sense my emotional shift, his gaze locking onto mine.

I take another deep breath, this time to calm down. "Why did you reset my mind? Maybe you can help me understand that part."

Paul settles back in his seat, but his uneasiness underscores what he said before. For his kind, there's an aspect of Russian roulette in just being around me. He deliberates for a moment. "I felt that, at least subconsciously, you needed to know what you are. For your own safety, you also needed to remain afraid."

I bark out an unexpected laugh. "I don't think you had anything to worry about there."

"You say that, but you might have overestimated your abilities. Simply put, you might have acted rashly." I get the feeling he's not telling me something, but he continues before I can think it through. "I also suspected that when your powers grew strong enough, you'd remember meeting me. As it turned out, that wasn't very long."

I sigh. "And here we are."

"And here we are," Paul agrees.

It's a strange moment—a bit more than surreal—as we sit there together like two old friends. Silent moments pass as I stare off across the room and collect my thoughts. Paul waits patiently but, then, it occurs to me that he's used to having vast spans of time at his disposal.

"You mentioned something before. A philosophical dispute, you called it. You said this was your region."

"That's true," Paul says.

"I need to ask a few questions."

Paul nods, somewhat wearily it seems. The impression I get is that he's prepared himself for this moment and isn't entirely sure of the outcome. Presumably, in persuading me, but the feeling I get is that it might involve something deeper, more troubling to consider.

"How are you any different from those others you've told me about? Aren't you essentially the same?"

"An intruder," he says. "A parasite."

Something in his eyes makes me glance away before I say, "Yes, that's what I mean. I need to know."

"Then I'll tell you," he says.

~~~

237

Paul tells me how, as the centuries passed, many of Vamanec P'yrin came to feel differently about their situation. Our race continued to evolve while they grew more empathetic. They could no longer leave—the means of returning home having been cut off—so they decided to exist differently. To survive, they found ways of procuring hosts just after the moment of natural death, when the consciousness natural to that body no longer resided within it. Paul spares me the details on most of this, but explains that they found ways of knowing when someone would die, as well as a window of time after death during which they could still claim a new host, past the point when anyone would be checking on the body.

The physical changes that took place afterward—the same changes that had always altered the bodies they claimed, imbuing them with vastly increased strength and agility, an intensely acute sense of smell, hearing and sight—almost always reversed what had caused the death to begin with. In essence, they survived by claiming what was no longer needed, the cost being that they subsisted with less than they would have physically desired to possess.

Another hour passes while I continue to ask questions that have kept building up inside me. Paul continues to answer. The old order which he'd alluded to had been held together according to ancient customs. There'd been no need for force or coercion among them. Ironically, the Vamanec P'yrin could do as they pleased with the lower inhabitants of this planet, but an old code made them respect what they regarded as natural authority among their own kind. Paul's leadership had been questioned only lately, as the other faction returned to believing it was their right to take what they wanted here, that they were essentially gods who could do as they pleased.

As our conversation draws to a close, I feel sure Paul is telling the truth. At least, in as much as my mind can accept any of what I've come to know. I save my most important questions for last.

"When you came here tonight, you knew there was a risk involved. Based on what you told me, you suspected I might have fully come into my powers. But you still came."

"I did," Paul says. "I was willing to take that risk."

"But you came alone. Why didn't Claudia come with you?"

I watch as what I've imagined impossible happens. His eyes glisten. "Because I couldn't allow myself to put her in that position. Despite everything we've discussed, I couldn't bring myself to do that."

And in that moment, I know. A feeling of certainty flows through me. "She's your daughter, isn't she?"

Paul's sad and ancient eyes remain on mine. "Yes, she is. Her name has changed a hundred times, at least. But Claudia is my daughter and always will be."

"Do you promise to keep protecting my mother and the other people I love? Even if I'm gone?"

Paul doesn't hesitate. "I promise."

When he says it, I believe him. What choice do I have? The fact is, while I thought he'd brought this fight to me that's not truly the case. This struggle came to me long ago, when Cassie was taken. But the conflict runs much deeper than that. It's in my history, my blood. And the time has finally come when this part of my history can't be ignored any longer.

CHAPTER 29

The next night is a Friday, exactly three weeks since the night when Ian went missing and I should have died. I stand alone, gazing out my apartment window at the neighborhood Justin and I chose to live in, wondering if I'll see it again tomorrow.

I came home earlier this afternoon, knowing it makes no difference now either way. If they wanted to find me, they could have by now, and after tonight it may not matter. Windows glow across the street, in other buildings where people go about their lives unaware of other worlds woven through their own. In one apartment, I watch as a young man crosses into his kitchen. He opens his refrigerator and gets something out—a can of soda or beer—then goes back to his living room where he sits and flips open his laptop. I wonder what he'd do if he knew what I know. That there are beings in this world who don't belong here, entities who can consume you if they wish or inhabit you if they prefer. I wonder what would happen if everyone knew that we've been invaded, occupied by an invisible enemy you could mistake for someone you've long known—your wife, your brother, your best friend.

Would there be panic in the streets, rioting and looting? Would people barricade themselves inside their homes, overcome with terror? Or would they go about things as they do now, outwardly calm as each day presents a new source of fear—terrorists, diseases, predators and psychopaths. There are monsters in this world accepted as being real, the existence of which we can't deny, and there are those we've chosen to stop believing in. If I'm to believe what Paul has told me, those monsters are mine alone to face. At least, for now.

I pick up my phone and once again think about calling my mother. But what would I tell her? That she might be about to lose me too, even now when I've survived another car crash? That she might not ever know. Or worse, that she might see me again and not even realize it wasn't me staring back at her? I put the phone down again.

Louie, always the empath, bounds through his door into the kitchen. I turn from the window as he pads toward me, his eye regarding me astutely. If anyone would know, Louie would. He slides himself along my calf and I kneel down to stroke his back and rub behind his ears.

"If I looked the same, but wasn't me, you'd know," I say. "Wouldn't you, boy?"

He purrs, raising his face to the ceiling.

"If someone took my body and came into this apartment, I bet you'd never bring them one single gift. That would be the end of that, right?"

Louie arches his back and caresses my leg with his body again.

"If I was invisible to everyone else, would you see me?"

As if to see if I'm poking fun at him, he peers up at my face with his one eye.

"I *know* it's a good eye," I whisper. "It's a *very* good eye. A hunter's eye."

Louie agrees, apparently, since he takes that as his cue to strut off again. I wipe a tear from my cheek as I watch him go, his tail sticking into the air and his graceful legs striding forward. A moment later, the cat door clatters in the kitchen again. He's gone hunting and it's time for me to do the same.

~~~

The thought came to me last night when I realized that today would be Friday. It seems nearly inconceivable, given what followed their last gathering, that they'd meet in the same place again, never mind on the same night of the week. But Paul has emphasized their arrogance and recklessness, how they don't fear being noticed. Just the opposite, in fact. As far as they're concerned, they own this world and its inhabitants. We're a lower life form, there only for exploitation and the guarantee of continued survival. If meeting at Fusion is a Friday night ritual for them, they'd see no need to change their plans.

The biggest thing working in my favor is that they can't be sure I know what I am. Horrifying, traumatizing things have happened to me, things that I should have no way of explaining. Ian and I were attacked, our minds ensnared. Ian killed our attacker, but then later turned on me. Presuming Haley returned to the fold following our encounter—either in Ian's body or that of another—she'd definitely report that I'd tried standing up to her. At the same time, she'd easily turned the tables, leaving me broken and left for dead. Now, my actions are a gamble—but, then, all of this is a gamble. As far as I can see, right now I have no choice but to bet on their arrogance and repugnant entitlement while I still can.

I circle the block until I find a parking space across the street, one with a clear view of the opening to the alley. I watch as people come and go. It seems strange that now, when I'm in the deepest shit of my life, I think of Ian and not Justin. But in a short time my reality has been flipped upside down. Justin has nothing to do with this world that I'm now a part of and, while I'm glad of that, they've also stolen my memories, made them fade too soon. About this, I'm seriously pissed off. I can't get those memories back, never as they once were. But right now I don't have time for the past. All I have is one chance to possibly save Rachel and maybe get a step closer to saving my sister.

"Ian, come on, buddy," I whisper. "I need a psychic flash right now. Are they in there? Yes or no?"

The answer may only come from within, but I still get an answer. The back of my neck has started to tingle, a low level charge to spark within my veins. It courses outward as it starts to thrum through me. This is instinct talking and I listen. They're in there, for sure. I feel it. I reach out again, to the weakened specter I spoke to last night. Again, I whisper. "Rachel, wherever you are, you need to hear me. Come back from the gray place. Stay close and remember what I told you."

I can't wait for an answer, hoping the connection we established is enough. I need to focus. I check the time to see that it's a little after ten, about when their gathering broke up last time. With any luck, they're consistent in the time spent on their meetings, whatever they're about. My heartbeat thuds in my ears as I imagine scenarios that might be about to unfold. I think about what Paul said, that they can choose not to "evict" the host entity—his or her soul or essence. No matter how it's phrased, the thought still sickens and terrifies me. His words come back to me. *They become somewhat intertwined.* If another person was locked within the occupied body, would I be able to sense it somehow? How could I possibly eject one and not the other?

Maybe I notice something in my peripheral vision, or maybe it's the agitation I already feel suddenly surging. Either way, I look to see that people have started to emerge from the alley. Under the streetlight glow, they carry themselves with confidence. I remember the charismatic allure that rippled through the room as Opal and her sect strode through it like rock stars. I get out of the car and cross the street to the sidewalk, feeling small and invisible. Nothing like Paul's claim that I'm an evolutionary throwback, a being with supernatural powers of my own. Still, my nerves crackle as I enter the alley, this time bumping my shoulder against the arm of a man who breaks his stride only long enough to regain momentum. He's gone a moment later, but the encounter sets my skin to buzzing, heat building inside me.

The alley is dark, the only light coming from the flashing neon arrow pointing toward the bar entrance. I take a deep breath and walk forward, toward a group of women walking in my direction. It's Opal and her entourage. There are four of them this time and I wonder if one could be Haley. I desperately hope not as I think of what that might mean. They're engaged in conversation, heads turned toward each other as their laughter slaps against brick. I don't hear their words, instead only the pounding of my own heart. The light of the sign flashes against wet walls, illuminating me.

One stops, her eyes glowing with neon reflection. The others shift their attention my way too. I stop, blocking their path, trying not to tremble.

The one with Rachel's face glances at each of her friends, then locks her gaze on me. She smirks and says, "Well, hello, human."

In the light of day, under other circumstances, it could seem a warm, humorous greeting or a flippant, ironic comment. In this dark alley, as I face the four of them, it's a cold statement of fact. They know that and laugh. What remains to be seen is whether I get the joke.

And I do. I totally get the joke. I get the fucking joke so much more than she could ever imagine. Because it tells me that she doesn't know. Haley hedged her bets and ran off.

I force myself to look into stolen eyes even as sweat trickles down my rib cage, right across my dragonfly. I muster every ounce of courage I have and smirk right back at her. "How's it going, Opal?"

Her expression shifts from one of haughty amusement to shock. "How do you know that name?"

"That's her," one of the friends says.

"Haley killed her," another one says. "That's what I heard."

My mind reels but I keep my eyes locked on Opal. "As it turns out, I can't actually die right now. Weird, huh? How about you?"

She steps back. "I'm not her, okay? I'm not who you're looking for."

I can't hold the current within me anymore. I wouldn't even if I could but I have no choice. I hold out my hands, fingers spread, the orb pulsing.

Her eyes widen against that glow. "Seriously, I'm not Opal! I swear, I'm not her."

Her friends scatter, moving so fast that I barely notice as they run to escape the alley. It's just the two of us now and it's also just her in there. Somehow, I know. I instinctively feel it. If she was human, I'd swear she wasn't lying. But the thing is, she's not human and I'm on fire.

"But you're not Rachel either, are you?" I say.

Her lips part but no words come out. There isn't time, because the orb doesn't float up or gracefully expand this time. Instead, it shoots from my hands and plunges through the woman across from me, punching through her sternum. She stares into my eyes as the horror of what's been unimaginable for so long overtakes her. Then, her eyes roll back and she collapses to the asphalt.

CHAPTER 30

I kneel next to her as water from a puddle seeps cold through my jeans at the knee and my heart pounds in my ears. She remains still, her face slack and lifeless, pale hands limp at her sides. I stare as the flashing neon sign intermittently lights up her face, casting its glow against the symbols tattooed upon her neck. Suddenly, she bucks against the asphalt, gasping for air. Her eyes pop open and she gazes up at me. I wait for recognition. When it shows, I still don't trust it.

"I know you," she says. "I remember talking to you."

I want to believe her but how can I?

"Who am I?" I say. "What's my name?"

"Autumn. You're Autumn."

Of course, that's not nearly enough. "Do you remember what happened?"

Her forehead creases with confusion. "I don't know. I... I'm not sure. I was in the gray place and then I was here. Where am I? What's going on?"

Tears stream from her eyes but I can't be sure they're real or who's causing them. I remember Ian driving the car, the stop light, shattered glass and hands upon my neck.

"I told you something," I say. "Do you remember?"

Her eyes search mine, quivering back and forth. She opens her mouth to speak but then shakes her head. The fact is, she could be anyone. I have no idea who's looking out at me from behind those eyes. I get to my feet, wait another moment, then turn away and start walking. I'm almost to where the alley opens onto the street when I hear her voice.

"Autumn?"

I stop and wait.

"I think I remember," she says. "You told me a secret."

I turn and walk back toward her as she raises herself up on her elbows. She waits until I get close to her again and then speaks softly. "It was about your sister," she says.

I nod and keep my eyes on hers.

"She used to call you Buttercup," she says. "When you were kids."

I hesitate once more, then kneel next to her. "Why?"

"Because of the show you watched together. The Powerpuff Girls. She said you were the tough one, like Buttercup. That's what you told me to remember."

My eyes fill and I blink away tears as a smile spreads across my face. I reach out and take her hand. "What's your name?"

"Rachel. My name is Rachel. Can you help me?"

"Yes I can," I say, "Come on, Rachel, let's get you home."

I help her get to her feet and she leans into me as we walk down the alley together. When we get to the street, Paul stands waiting beside my car.

CHAPTER 31

Before blowing out the candles, I close my eyes and make a wish, one I could never have imagined making before. When I open my eyes, I want everything to be the same. My mother will be sitting next to Molly and Daniel. Zach will be sitting next to Ellen. Zelda and Ethan will be fighting over who gets which crayon as they continue to color in the books my mother bought for them. I only wish that they'll still be the same people they were five seconds ago when I closed my eyes.

It's a simple wish, one that would have been impossible to conceive of at any time in the past. And while the odds are good—in fact, very good—the fact is there aren't any guarantees. People go missing. They suddenly disappear. It happens all the time, every day. And the sad truth is that, most of the time, they never come back. Which, I guess, is part of why we stay plugged into those news stories. Because our gut instinct tells us there's a very strong chance that the missing person will never be found. We hope and we pray that we're wrong. Quite often, though, we're right. But there's also something else I know now, something I'm glad those around me don't. The other part of why we focus on those stories. Because, in some distant part of our collective memory, we remember something we were told to forget.

I open my eyes and blow out the candles as those around me clap and laugh. I fan away waxy smoke.

"How old are you now?" Zelda says.

"Twenty-eight," I say.

Her eyes widen. "That's really old."

"I'm basically an old lady now."

Zelda giggles. "No, you're not!"

Ethan stares to see if I could possibly be telling the truth. "You're not old," he says. "Dad's old!"

I cup my hand at my ear and do an old lady voice. "What? Speak up, I can't hear you."

Zelda laughs again.

Ethan shakes his head and says, "I don't get it."

Zelda shoots him a look. "She's being old. Old people can't hear well."

"Dad hears okay," Ethan says.

Zach cups his ear too. "What?"

Zelda and Ellen exchange glances and both turn to look at my mother.

She narrows her eyes. "I can hear you perfectly," she says.

"See, that means she's not old!" Ethan says.

"Exactly," my mother says.

I pretend not to notice as Zelda steals Ethan's red crayon, even though she has one of her own.

Ellen cuts the cake, placing slices on plates. Zach goes to get the ice cream from where he left it to soften on the counter. He digs a serving spoon into the container and brings it back to the table, licking a bit off of his finger. "The place looks great," my mother says, looking around. "You guys did a nice job."

"It really does," Ellen says. "I love the colors."

We sit in my tiny dining kitchen, which is now a pale shade of blue after all of these years being white. The living room is now a soft sage green. Zach helped me make it happen over the last couple of weeks. I meant to do it on my own but it just felt like time for some help. I've spent way too much time alone in this place thinking about the past. Not to mention, hanging around with ghosts. Not actual ghosts. Those aren't a problem at all. It's the other kind that I need to move on from, the ghosts within me that I only imagine still being there. It's just not fair of me not to let them move on, and I'm not being fair to myself.

Still, I wonder if Justin would like the changes we've made. *What do you think, Babe?* The feeling I get is that, yes, he'd like what we've done very much.

We eat our cake and I open my gifts, feeling self-conscious as people watch to see if I like what I've been given. New clothes and bath towels from my mother, sketch books and Prismacolor pencils from Molly and Daniel, a beautiful cut glass candle holders from Ellen. We laugh over the kids' gifts to me, adult coloring books and my own DVD copy of *Frozen*. Zach waits proudly for me to open his gift, which turns out to be a power drill.

"Autumn has skills," Zach says. "She just needed to believe in herself. Of course, it doesn't hurt having decent tools."

It's a sweet gesture, this vote of confidence, which resonates for me in a way I can't explain to them. It would seem that I do have skills. Now, I just need to sharpen them more and find a way to pass them on again, something my great-grandmother never got to do.

"When do I get a drill, Daddy?" Zelda says.

"I want a hammer!" Ethan says.

Ellen lifts an eyebrow. "Great. That'll be perfect. You two can reenact the Hunger Games."

Half an hour later, they leave. It's only nine o'clock, but it's also a Tuesday so they all have to get up in the morning. I tell myself I'm being foolish, that I should probably read or watch a show and then get to bed. But I decide to head out, to check once again. Like Zach said, I have skills. I just need to keep believing in myself.

~~~

Penny's face brightens as I walk through the door. She's working the bar tonight, more than likely the floor too since a quick glance shows it to be a slow night. A few people sit in the booths and there's just a few more at the bar.

"Hey, stranger." Penny slides a cocktail napkin in front of me. "Watcha having, cerveza or vino?"

The funny thing is, despite it being my birthday neither sounds good right now. "Maybe just some tea."

Penny arches an eyebrow in surprise. At the same time, the corner of her mouth lifts in a smile. "It's a good night for tea," she says. "Kind of nippy out there."

She brings me my tea and we chat for a few minutes before she wanders off to empty the glasswasher. As my tea steeps my eyes occasionally flit over to the corner of the bar where I first spotted Ian watching me. It's probably foolish, but I keep thinking he'll find me somewhere we both knew together, either at my apartment, here or at his cabin. I've returned there several times now even though I'd have a difficult time explaining my presence. Ian's not dead, though. I just know it somehow.

Come on, Ian. We're not done yet. Where are you?

I think about what Paul told me after we dropped Rachel off on the outskirts of her neighborhood, her mind reset both to erase the horror and because no one would ever believe her. The one I'd thought was named Opal had been telling the truth. She wasn't who Paul was looking for. He didn't say how he knew and I didn't ask. At the time, I was afraid to. His anger was palpable, like something coiled and dangerous, which in my heightened state felt like sparks crackling against my skin. Within moments, Claudia pulled up driving Paul's Mercedes. "I'm sure I'll see you again," he said. Then he got out of the car and they drove off together.

I get the feeling someone is watching me and I look around. Eyes meet mine in the back-bar mirror. It takes a moment but he raises his glass and I recognize him. A moment later, Ed settles in beside me and I still think he looks too young to be here.

"Autumn, right?"

"That's right," I say. "I heard they found your friend last week."

He nods, his expression somewhere between confused and relieved. "I haven't seen her yet. I don't think anyone has. Other than her family, I mean."

Ed's confusion is understandable, his viewpoint the same as that expressed by the media. The headlines proclaimed relief at the lost girl being found while the articles went on to state that not much more was known, that updates would be forthcoming. So far, there hasn't been much in the way of updates.

"They say she has amnesia," Ed says. "That she doesn't remember anything."

I nod and take a sip of tea. "That's what I heard too. Strange, isn't it."

"Really strange. I heard she might have joined a cult or something."

Of course, social media had been full of speculation. I heard the part about the cult too. It was the only reason people could think of to explain why she'd returned looking so different, her hair cut short, her body leaner and inexplicably stronger. One report said she'd even grown taller and I wondered if it could be somehow possible. Someone had managed to get a photo of the mysterious tattoo on Rachel's neck, which had been making the rounds too.

"Well, I'm glad she's okay," I say.

"Me too." Ed tries to smile, not quite pulling it off. I understand. He has feelings for Rachel and now he's not sure what to think. No one is. "Hey, can I buy you a drink? You got the last round."

I raise my cup of tea. "Maybe next time but thank you."

Ed gestures to where a couple of other guys sit farther down the bar. "I should probably get back to my friends. Nice seeing you again."

After he's gone, I spend a little more time catching up with Penny as she comes and goes. She tells me she's seeing someone new, a guy she met at a Reiki class she's been going to. She doesn't mention her ex-husband once so I guess, between the Reiki and the new guy in her life, things for Penny are starting to look up. I'm happy for her and, while it's nice seeing her, being here isn't doing me any good. Besides, if I know Louie, he'll have been waiting for everyone to leave before bringing me my birthday present. Another dead mouse or bird. Just what I always wanted. Still, it's nice imagining that someone out there in the world might be thinking of me tonight.

I ride the bus home alongside no ghosts and just a few other living people, those still out for some reason on a Tuesday night after ten. I look out the window at the passing lights of townhouses and apartment buildings, thinking about all those people who have no way of knowing what I know. Part of me would give anything to trade places, while part of me thinks it's better to know that monsters are real. After all, you can't fight something you think doesn't exist.

At the last stop before my own, footsteps sound from the back of the bus. A woman walks past and a slip of paper flutters into my lap, folded into a tight square. I look up as she descends the steps to get off the bus, her face covered by a veil of dark hair.

"Excuse me," I say. "You dropped this."

The woman turns to look. Her lips curl up in a smile as her eyes meet mine, eyes I've looked into a thousand times before. She's older and taller and in so many other ways almost unrecognizable. All the same, I'd know my sister anywhere.

She gets off, the door closes and the bus keeps moving.

If you enjoyed this book, please leave a review! Your reviews allow independently published books like this one to find new readers. Don't worry, your review doesn't have to be long either—just a paragraph or a couple of sentences is just fine and it will really make a big difference. Thank you!

Watch for *In the Blood: Realm Watchers Book 2.* **Coming soon!**

Acknowledgments

Special thanks to Carmen Repsold, Patti Winters, Jennifer Mantura, Tamara Ingram, Diane Changala, Tina Fulkerson, Vicki McCreary, Shawnee Kostal, Dru Bennett, Debi Deason, Deborah MacArthur, Lacey Lane, Lori Kis, Susan Warr and Kendra Moll for beta-reading, catching edits and giving me the confidence to publish this rather strange book. You guys are the best, and I really appreciate your time and efforts! Many thanks also to Kim, Darja and Milo at Deranged Doctor Design for creating the book covers for this series.

About J. S. Malcom

J. S. Malcom is the author of the Realm Watchers urban fantasy series, of which Autumn Winters is just the beginning. J. S. lives in Richmond, Virginia, a town full of history and ghosts (not to mention, many other supernatural creatures, including Autumn and Cassie).

51766284R00166

Made in the USA
San Bernardino, CA
31 July 2017